Christopher Pike

The Star Group

AN ARCHWAY PAPERBACK
Published by POCKET BOOKS
New York London Toronto Sydney Tokyo Singapore

The sale of this book without its cover is unauthorized. If you purchased
this book without a cover, you should be aware that it was reported to
the publisher as "unsold and destroyed." Neither the author nor the
publisher has received payment for the sale of this "stripped book."

This book is a work of fiction. Names, characters, places and
incidents are products of the author's imagination or are used
fictitiously. Any resemblance to actual events or locales or persons,
living or dead, is entirely coincidental.

AN ARCHWAY PAPERBACK *Original*

An Archway Paperback published by
POCKET BOOKS, a division of Simon & Schuster Inc.
1230 Avenue of the Americas, New York, NY 10020

Copyright © 1997 by Christopher Pike

All rights reserved, including the right to reproduce
this book or portions thereof in any form whatsoever.
For information address Pocket Books, 1230 Avenue
of the Americas, New York, NY 10020

ISBN: 0-671-55057-8

First Archway Paperback printing December 1997

10 9 8 7 6 5 4 3 2 1

AN ARCHWAY PAPERBACK and colophon are
registered trademarks of Simon & Schuster Inc.

Cover art by Franco Accornero

Printed in the U.S.A.

IL 9+

I'm not. My mind

That's the reason for writing my story, to try to make people understand. But I doubt whether anyone will ever read it, that I'll even be given a chance to finish it. My sticky blood will splatter the computer screen, my shattered head will fall on the keyboard. I try not to think about it, but it is all I can focus on. What I am trying to stop has almost unlimited power. As I eye the gun, there is a tiny part of me that fears that the power has already been used on me.

You see, the gun has blood on it.

130740

DATE DUE

DEC. 29. 20		
MAY 18 2001		
APR 27 '02		
MAY 16 '02		
MAY 31 '02		
OCT 25 '02		
Nov 11		
MAY 27 '03		
UL 08 '03		
AUG 26 '03		
AUG 26 '04		
MAR 29 '05		
JAN 2 4 '08		

#47-0108 Peel Off Pressure Sensitive

Books by Christopher Pike

BURY ME DEEP
CHAIN LETTER 2
DIE SOFTLY
THE ETERNAL ENEMY
EXECUTION OF INNOCENCE
FALL INTO DARKNESS
FINAL FRIENDS #1: THE PARTY
FINAL FRIENDS #2: THE DANCE
FINAL FRIENDS #3: THE GRADUATION
GIMME A KISS
THE IMMORTAL
LAST ACT
THE LAST VAMPIRE
THE LAST VAMPIRE 2: BLACK BLOOD
THE LAST VAMPIRE 3: RED DICE
THE LAST VAMPIRE 4: PHANTOM
THE LAST VAMPIRE 5: EVIL THIRST
THE LAST VAMPIRE 6: CREATURES OF FOREVER
THE LOST MIND
MASTER OF MURDER
THE MIDNIGHT CLUB
MONSTER
REMEMBER ME
REMEMBER ME 2: THE RETURN
REMEMBER ME 3: THE LAST STORY
ROAD TO NOWHERE
SCAVENGER HUNT
SEE YOU LATER
SPELLBOUND
THE STAR GROUP
THE STARLIGHT CRYSTAL
THE TACHYON WEB
TALES OF TERROR #1
THE VISITOR
WHISPER OF DEATH
THE WICKED HEART
WITCH

Available from ARCHWAY Paperbacks

For orders other than by individual consumers, Pocket Books grants a discount on the purchase of **10 or more** copies of single titles for special markets or premium use. For further details, please write to the Vice-President of Special Markets, Pocket Books, 1633 Broadway, New York, NY 10019-6785, 8th Floor.

For information on how individual consumers can place orders, please write to Mail Order Department, Simon & Schuster Inc., 200 Old Tappan Road, Old Tappan, NJ 07675.

For Nellie

CHAPTER

1

I have a loaded gun on my desk beside my computer. A stainless-steel .357 magnum Ruger revolver, four copper hollow points in five steel chambers—my friend's gun. I'm thinking of using it, before the sun comes up. Thinking of putting it in my mouth and pulling the trigger—as soon as I get my story down. But I'm not depressed or suicidal or anything like that. I don't want to die. I have never wanted to see the sun rise so much in my life, but I'm afraid that if I don't move on, to another plane, many people on Earth will die. I sound like a cult fanatic, I know. But I'm not. My mind has never been so clear. That's the reason for writing my story, to try to make people understand. But I doubt whether anyone will ever read it, that I'll even be given a chance to finish it. My sticky blood will splatter the computer screen, my shattered head will fall on the keyboard. I try not to think about it, but it is all I can focus on. What I am trying to stop has almost unlimited power. As I eye the gun, there is a tiny part of me that fears that the power has already been used on me.

You see, the gun has blood on it.

My name is Daniel Stevens and I am eighteen years old. One week ago I graduated from La Mirada High, in Orange County, California. I think it was the last day of school that it started, but of course I know that can't be. It started before I was born, before any of us came to this planet.

I remember waking the morning of that last day of school with a smile on my face, something I never do. Maybe I'd been dreaming about Gale Schrater, the girl I had loved since the beginning of time. I had made up my mind the previous night to ask Gale for her phone number, before it was too late, before I never saw her again. There was something about it being the end of school that empowered me. If she said no I would never have to see her again. Still, if she said no, I knew I would die.

I had to get up early. A couple of buddies of mine, Sal Barry and James Yearn, planned to start the big day surfing. Jimmy was supposed to pick me up at five, and my clock said it was ten after five right then. I got out of bed fast, anxious to get into the salt water. Jimmy pulled up as I walked out of my garage with my wet suit in one hand and my surfboard in the other. Jimmy drove a Ford station wagon that looked like it had backed into the sixties, but it could get us to the beach, twenty miles away, so I didn't care. My own car, a Toyota Corolla, was sitting in the garage and waiting for me to put in more time at the grocery store so I could afford to get it fixed. I didn't know what was wrong with it, except that it didn't run.

2

"I hear it's breaking big," Jimmy said as I strapped my stuff on his roof rack. My board was a six-foot Chuck Dent, the old wax so thick that it looked like something that had caught an infection. But there was no way I was going to scrape the stuff off; to me it was like a fragrant history of past good times. Coconut wax smelled great no matter how old it got. After I finished strapping on my board, I got in beside Jimmy. He was sipping from a thermos of coffee, couldn't function without the stuff.

"Then I should shoot the pier today," I said.

Jimmy was not enthusiastic about my trying even though he and Sal had shot the pier—rode a wave through the pier pilings—a thousand times. I was the only coward, but they were cool about it. I hadn't been surfing nearly as long, only a year, whereas Sal and Jimmy had owned boards since they were ten.

Jimmy was a burly guy, already going a little soft around the gut. But he was handsome as hell and more popular than any jock at school. He had dark good looks, a steel jaw, and what money he didn't lavish on his car he spent on clothes. But his main attraction was the way he moved. He had a special confidence, like a kid who had already left school, struck it rich, and only returned to make up a few classes. The teachers at La Mirada deferred to Jimmy, and he was so smooth, he never pushed it. What I mean was he was strong without being a jerk. We had been friends for four years, but he had only managed to talk me into surfing the previous year. Jimmy was probably my best friend, although Sal was a close second. Jimmy had already been accepted at UCLA, and I knew he was going places.

Me, I was a stick by comparison. I could eat two hamburgers at lunch for two months in a row and the animal fat would all turn to calcium, to bone. Not an ounce of fat on me. But I wasn't bad looking. My mother said all the women she played bingo with had crushes on me. I also had dark hair, which I had taken to wearing long and curly. It made me look like an artist, a writer, which I hoped to be at some future date. I loved writing stories in which I saved the world and Gale fell in love with me. I often fantasized about publishing a book with Gale in it, and being able to give her a signed copy.

"Today might not be the day to become a hero," Jimmy said as he put the car in gear and we rolled toward Beach Boulevard. There was hardly a tinge of light in the east, but we both knew Sal would already be at the beach and in the water. Sal had taken to living in his van the last month, ever since his stepfather had tried to hit him over the head with a crowbar. Sal was as black as ink but had a stepdad as rednecked as a firecracker—go figure. His mother liked to walk on the wild side. Sal's uneasy home life had him already thinking of joining the Marines, which Jimmy and I were trying to talk him out of. Sal had been our school's star quarterback and destined for a full scholarship at some plush university until he hurt his knee and missed the second half of the season. But it seemed the Marines thought his knee was strong enough to take a shot.

"Are you worried I'll kill myself?" I asked about Jimmy's not wanting me to shoot the pier.

"Nah. I just don't want you to wreck my old

board." I had bought the board from Jimmy. He added, "I hear it's ten foot."

I was impressed, and a little scared. I had never ridden such big waves. I hoped someone somewhere was exaggerating, as often was the case when it came to waves. Yet I felt that it was likely I would risk my life. I knew Jimmy was more worried about me than his board.

"Had any tests yesterday?" I asked.

Jimmy yawned. "Calculus final. But even if I flunked it I should still get an A in the class."

"I had a test in history. If I got an A on it, I still only get a B in the class. I don't even know if I'll show up today. Don't want to know how I did."

Jimmy nodded. "No one's going to be in classes much today. Me, I'm going to try to take a nap after school, before the ceremony. You know we'll probably be up all night."

The all-night graduation party was at Disneyland. Our senior class along with probably two dozen others would be there. The word was that Disneyland would be kept open until three in the morning. I was hoping to talk to Gale there, maybe share a ride with her. It wasn't as though we never talked, we actually shared history class. It was just that I was clearly in the nice-guy-friend class. Most girls at school saw me that way, I was sad to admit.

I asked my next question carefully.

"Is Shena going?"

Jimmy stared straight ahead out the window. "I don't know."

"You haven't talked to her?"

"It's hard to talk to Shena these days," Jimmy said.

Until six months ago Shena Adams had been Jimmy's girlfriend, a blond cutie. They were inseparable, always together. But it was too bad they were together last Christmas Eve. That was the night the battery in Jimmy's car blew up in Shena's face and sprayed her with acid. The wounds had healed, but the scars would never disappear, even with extensive plastic surgery, which was still planned. Her nickname at school was *Toast*—adolescents can be so kind. The accident, according to Shena, had been Jimmy's fault. He was such a cool guy, he refused to talk about it. I took his silence as virtue. I liked to give my friends the benefit of the doubt.

"How's she feeling?" I asked.

"I think, physically, she has no more pain," Jimmy said. "But emotionally she's still way down. Little things get to her. Today we'll all be photographed, and she can't stop thinking about how she'll look."

"She can always stand in the back with nerds like me."

"I doubt she'll even go to the ceremony."

"That would be a shame," I said.

Jimmy wanted to change the subject. "Are you going to ask Gale out today?"

"Yeah. If the pier pilings don't restructure my skull."

"I know Gale's going to Disneyland. I was talking to Sal, I think she's going with Teri."

Teri, Teresa Jettison, was Sal's girlfriend, one of the smartest girls in the school.

I gulped. "I didn't think they were close."

Jimmy smiled. "Maybe Gale just wants to go with Teri so she can get to you."

"Things like that don't happen in the real world." I added, "I really am going to ask her out."

"How's your pyromaniac story going?" Jimmy asked.

"Great. My hero just burned down half of Malibu. He's about to steal a gasoline truck; he's in seventh heaven."

Jimmy shook his head. "I don't see how you can sit still and write so many words. Doesn't your brain get tired?"

"It gets tired when I don't write." I added, "I've also started on an alien story."

"I didn't know you liked sci-fi."

"It doesn't feel like sci-fi to me. It's more like supernatural."

"What's it about?" Jimmy asked.

"I don't know."

Jimmy snorted. "How can you write a story if you don't know what it's about?"

I shifted uneasily. The story had been plaguing me, it was true, yet I didn't really know what the central idea was. I just had several images bouncing around in my brain: a wide meadow surrounded by purple trees; a blue sun and a red sun burning in the sky together; a group of people, who were not really people, talking about the fate of our world. Yet none of these images was the reason it felt like a supernatural story to me. It was the *feel* of the story—it didn't have a scientific explanation behind it. What the group was talking about was not science. It was spiritual.

"Sometimes I just make up things as I go along," I said.

"Do you ever get stuck? And all your work is wasted?"

"Sometimes." I added, "But on this story I'm not going to get stuck."

"What's it called?" Jimmy asked.

"'The Star Group.'"

"It's a short story?"

"I have to see how it develops. I haven't got all the characters yet."

Of course, I didn't know then that I was plotting my epitaph. That Mentor was already on to me, inside me, directing me toward the inevitable. How many dreams are real? How many nightmares chase our shadows? I felt cold as I answered Jimmy's questions, and I hadn't even gotten into the ocean yet. The endless black ocean all around us, beyond the world. For most people, nightmares are born in the dark. But ours was born deep inside my skull.

CHAPTER

2

The sun was close to rising when we parked at the beach. I really loved to be out on the water when the sun touched the horizon, east or west. At those moments my breath would be suspended for several seconds, and I would feel myself become expanded, connected to the cosmos, as if a clock deep inside me had just turned with the Earth. Marked off another round of life and recorded it for all time. Then I would think of Gale, and how short life really was. For an eighteen-year-old I was incredibly fatalistic. For example, I honestly could not say I loved Gale because I didn't really know her. Yet I felt that was the only way I could love her, as an icon to mystery, something I could ultimately never touch. I wanted her but I was afraid to have her. Or maybe I was just afraid. Yeah, I enjoyed sunrises more than sunsets. Stars came in the dark, and even before the madness they had me spooked.

We found Sal fetching his board by the pier. A monster wash of white water had already snapped his

9

leash on the board. I didn't have to look out at the huge breakers to know what an awesome day it was. Sal's face said it all. His leash was broken, but he was in ecstasy. His white teeth glistened in his black face. The salt water on his lips was tasting good to him. He was not handsome like Jimmy, but magnetic still. Sal looked as if he were from another time, a powerful tribal leader, who carried a board instead of a spear. He surfed like a warrior, man against nature, not against man. He regularly shot the pier and defied the sea to crush him against the concrete pillars.

I think we shared that, a not too deeply buried death wish, and that brought us close. I mean, I was a nobody at school and Sal was a football hero, although a wounded one. There was no reason he should hang out with me, except one—he liked me. I considered our bond an alchemy of unknown forces. I wasn't from the same world as he was—my parents were sweet folks who never fought—and yet we fit perfectly together. Often, out on the water, Sal seemed to read my mind. He always knew when I was thinking of Gale. But unlike Jimmy, he wasn't sure if I should ask her out. He wasn't convinced it was better to have loved and lost than not to have loved at all. If he joined the Marines, he knew, he wouldn't see Teri again. She cared a great deal for him, but she was not going to wait for him and throw away her scholarship to Berkeley. Except for a B in one class, PE, Teri would have been our class valedictorian. Like Jimmy, Teri was going places, and Sal was wise enough to know he might be left behind. Perhaps he wanted to get out while the getting was good.

"Today is the day," Sal said as he dragged himself

and his board onto the shore. "I've never ridden waves like these."

I watched as a twelve-foot monster struck the end of the pier and sent up a sheet of spray. Even the people on the pier were getting soaked, marveling at the fools who would dare surf such creatures. There were very few people in the water; there would be no traffic.

"I've never *seen* waves like these," I mumbled, echoing Sal.

Sal considered as he stared at the surf. "Maybe you should take the day off, Daniel."

I shook my head. "Today I shoot the pier."

Sal laughed. "I tried that and chickened out at the last second. Wait till the waves get below four feet."

Jimmy nodded. "There are three breaks today. Haven't seen that in years."

Sal held up his broken leash. It had snapped in the middle, almost exactly in two. "It's hell getting out," he said. "I guess I've got to hold on to my board for the rest of the day."

"Will the lifeguards be out today?" Jimmy asked as he put a foot in the water. He was already squeezing into his wet suit. We all wore them, short jobs that covered our torsos, but only half our legs and arms. They were more comfortable than full suits. Sal shook his head at Jimmy's question.

"The red flags are up," Sal said. "The lifeguards won't be on duty today. It's your own fault if you drown."

"Has anyone disappeared?" Jimmy asked.

Sal frowned. "I heard somebody out there was looking for his buddy."

"Maybe he'll show up," I said.

"Maybe," Sal said.

We got in the water and started paddling out. We were lucky, we caught a break in the sets. But even without the waves pounding in, I could feel the energy in the water. A thousand backwashes trying to settle against one another. And on the horizon, still a quarter of a mile out, I saw blue walls. My heart was pounding. I was scared, but I was having a great time.

The waves came. They swelled beneath my board like elephants preparing to charge. I let the first set go by, I wanted to get in my rhythm. Jimmy was bold. He launched himself into the last wave of the set and we heard him scream as his head disappeared down the back side of the mountain, heading south, away from the pier. Sal and I watched as the wave exploded in a fury of white. But Jimmy had played it smart and pulled out immediately after going over the falls. He paddled back toward us wearing the same crazy grin as Sal.

"That was intense!" he shouted.

"What's it feel like going down?" I asked.

"Like you're falling ten stories," Jimmy said, pulling up beside us to catch his breath.

"You've got to dive away from your board if the wall comes over you," Sal told me. "If your board hits you wrong today, it could cut you in two."

I nodded. "I'm riding the next one."

"Don't take anything unless you're positioned perfectly," Sal warned.

His last comment I took to heart. I was out of place for the next wave, but the one after that had my name on it, maybe the name from my tombstone. It was an easy twelve-footer. As I turned my back to it and began to paddle, began to feel it pick me up, I felt as if I were in the grip of Mother Nature Herself.

The speed of the wave was incredible, I was paddling as fast as I could and it was going to sweep me by. Not sure what to do, I jumped up and forced the tip of my board down. For a moment I was pointed almost straight down, and all of a sudden I knew what Jimmy meant about the ten stories. The foam churning below me looked like the bubbling brew in a distant landscape. I had jumped out of a plane without a parachute. The wave suddenly seemed ten times its height. I had caught it, or it had caught me, I wasn't sure yet.

But I didn't have a chance to worry about it. I was going down fast, screaming my head off, a blue wall grinding out the daylight on my right. The breath of the wave was on me, the fine spray of seawater. Even before its fist blew me into chaos, I felt it winding up. One second a liquid tube was gracefully curling over my head, and the next I was flying into a washing machine broken on the spin cycle. The wave didn't merely close over my head, it slammed the door shut on top of it. I was forced down, hard and deep.

Fortunately I had a decent breath in my lungs, and my arms over my head. While being tossed in the roller coaster, my board tried to attack me twice, but it only ended up bruising my back. I estimated that the wave held me down forty seconds—a long time to stay submerged in a swimming pool, but an eternity in a roaring ocean. Yet I didn't panic, even when the pain started to grow inside my chest. It was my last day of school, the first day of my love affair with Gale. I simply could not die, it would be too unfair.

When I came up I was close to shore; my leash had snapped as well. My board was bumping the sand, some little kid was picking it up and showing his friends. I waved to my pals to let them know I was OK and went for my board. The kid looked at me like he wanted a dollar for finding my board. I gave him a smile, I was feeling pretty good. My ride had been a total disaster and yet now I had the confidence to go for it. I really was going to try to shoot the pier.

When I reached Sal, Jimmy was already screaming his head off on another wave. Sal pulled a lighter and a pack of cigarettes out from under his wet suit. He kept his goods in a plastic Baggie. He often smoked while he was out on the water, no one knew how he managed. We were both sitting up on our boards when he lighted up.

"How did it feel?" he asked.

"I bought it big time. But it was cool."

He nodded as he blew smoke, staring off in the distance. Sal loved the nature as much as the surfing. I think he used the sport as an excuse to get close to the elements. His muscles shone in the breaking light. The sun had risen while I was almost drowning. Sal sighed as his face became more thoughtful.

"I love this," he said.

I nodded. "It's a great day."

He shook his head. "It's always a great day when you're out on the water with your buddies."

"You're just feeling nostalgic because school ends today."

"Maybe." He seemed sad. "I keep feeling like it's all going to end soon."

"But we'll surf all summer."

"That's not what I mean." He changed the subject abruptly. "I don't know what Jimmy's going to do with Shena."

"What can he do? It's done." I paused. "Does he want to break up with her?"

"You know better. They *are* broken up, they just haven't admitted it to themselves yet. At least Jimmy hasn't. Shena might already know it's hopeless."

The words were hard to hear. I liked Shena, she had been our class homecoming queen. Now she was just—Toast. God, how I hated that nickname.

"Just because her face is a mess?" I asked.

Sal shook his head. "Jimmy cares for her just the same. But Shena knows how people react to her face, no matter what they say to her. She's not a phony, she knows looks aren't everything, but still she can't be who she was with all those scars. I don't think anyone could."

"But that's all the more reason they should stay together. They need each other."

Sal eyed me, he had a way of looking right through me at times like this.

"You're a romantic idiot. The someday-future-love you think is going to solve all your problems doesn't exist."

I was hurt. "You just say that because you already miss Teri. Because you're such an idiot you think you have to join the Marines and leave her."

He savored his cigarette. "I just have no illusions. You do, you think what we decide today matters in the long run. Why, in ten years I doubt we'll even know each other. You'll be a famous writer; Jimmy will be a congressman; Teri will be the head of a corporation; and I'll be working in some factory, telling stories about how great I used to be at football."

"You don't even talk about football nowadays."

"That's my point, I might sink low as life goes on. Who knows?" He looked at the water. "That's why I love right now, it's real."

"You're depressing me."

Sal laughed and put out his cigarette in the water and placed the stub back in his Baggie. He never littered, he was very conscientious.

"Let's ride a wave together," he said. "I want to see what you're made of."

Another set came, monsters all of them. As was often the case, the third wave looked the biggest. Sal waited for it and I waited for Sal. With our backs to the wave, the pier was on our left. Slowly we moved into position. Jimmy was trying to get back out but was having trouble. Sal's words continued to bother me for reasons I couldn't pinpoint. Sal didn't do all that well at school, but he was deep. When he spoke, I listened.

Sal was on my right. He would cut to the right, and he figured I would follow him. But I had other ideas. As the third wave began to swell beneath us, I pointed my board to the left and started paddling frantically. In front of me was the pier, the concrete pillars covered with many years of barnacle pilings, so sharp they could cut like razors. Coming hard at my back was a wave that was at least fifteen feet high. As it picked me up, I had a momentary feeling of being on top of the world. I stood quickly, feeling the power. A part of me was absolutely terrified, another part had never felt so invincible. Sal shouted something behind me but I didn't catch it. It was probably *Stop!*

I screamed as I whipped down the face of the wave, then I laughed. Overhead, out the corner of my eye, I saw two dozen people on the pier shout and point at me. The wave was so high, the top of my head was only ten feet under the floor of the pier. The spray of the wave showered my face. Beneath my feet my board felt like a runaway torpedo. The lip of the wave began to curl over my head, and the blue tube I entered right then was a thing of dreams, all encompassing. Only dead in front of me was daylight visible, and in the center of that light were three tall cement pillars. I couldn't turn away from them; I didn't have the control. The wave itself would have to save me. If the tube closed, my life would slam shut with it because I couldn't wipe out, not in this surf and expect to survive a roll through the pier. The only way to live was to make it to the other side. The razor edge of my existence, of my mortality, filled me with a strange intoxication. Maybe my death wish was more vital than I realized.

I shot the pier. I missed the pillars by inches, and when I emerged on the other side the tube opened up and the sun shone on my face. That wave, possibly the biggest wave of the day, I rode almost all the way to shore. When I climbed out of the water and walked back to the south side of the pier, Sal and Jimmy were waiting for me on the shore. They had both witnessed my ride, the whole pier had. They just looked at me and shook their heads and patted me on the back. We didn't go back in the water, it wasn't necessary for us to do any more that morning. We didn't even speak about what I had done. What had happened was the best—it couldn't be topped. And in a sense we had all shared in it. Right then I felt closer to my friends than I ever had. I loved them, even more than I loved my own life. Maybe that was why I'd been able to risk my life, in a strange way, for them.

CHAPTER

3

After showering and driving to school with Sal, I collected my yearbook and searched it for pictures of myself and Gale. There were none of me, of course, except my senior picture, but there were four of my love: Gale sitting by herself on a bench; Gale talking to an art teacher; Gale laughing with the cheerleaders; Gale taking a nap on the grass behind a building.

The last picture made my heart pound. What would it be like to nap beside her? My darling, I memorized each page number. I would have blown up the pictures if I could, I was thinking of looking into whether it was possible. Sick, yeah, I know.

Teresa Jettison, Teri, was the first one to sign my yearbook. She came up to me as I was drooling over Gale's photos, but I was quick to shut the book. Teri was dressed real nice in a grown-up sort of way. She was wearing a tan suit that made her look like the smart executive we all thought she was going to be. Teri had a knack for business. Already she owned a small mail-order company that imported cashmere blankets and shawls from Scotland and India and sold them to New Age clients for meditation and stuff like that. She was only eighteen, but she had made twenty thousand last year. And she was so nice and not the least bit conceited—she blew me away.

Being black, she had dark hair, and it was her hair that most intrigued me about her looks. It was shiny and fluttered around her head like living threads. She had a way of looking you right in the eye when you were talking to her, as if there was nothing that mattered to her except what you were saying. Her relationship with Sal pained her, no question, but she accepted the good with the bad and didn't whine. She gave me a big hug after she came up to me.

"I heard what you did," she said. "Nut. You could have died."

I smiled with pleasure. "Today is not a good day to die." I paused. "I like the picture of you and the clown. It looks like you have your hand up his nose."

Teri blushed. "That guy was hitting on me. I was trying to push him away. I can't believe Shena used that picture, I told her not to."

Earlier in the year Shena had been editor of the yearbook, but quit after her accident. Teri knew that. Shena probably had nothing to do with the clown picture. For sure, if Shena had been editor still, she would have put in a couple of pictures of me—not that I cared. I didn't photograph well; I think it's the light.

"It's still a sexy picture," I said.

Teri laughed. "Yeah. Dwarfs and clowns are in this year. I liked your picture."

"My one and only?"

"It's quality that counts." She gestured to my book. "Can I sign it?"

"Sure." We exchanged books. I opened hers to the clown picture and pulled out a pen. I wrote quickly, not sure what to say.

Teri,

You are one of my heroes. Don't let go of Sal, he is my other hero. Set the world on fire, I know you got the fire.

Love,

Daniel

She was taking her time writing in my book, and I wondered if I should have said more. I disliked butting in on other people's business, but I couldn't stand the thought of their breaking up. Or Shena and Jimmy for that matter. I was a hopeless romantic. Teri finally gave me back my book, but when I went to read her inscription she stopped me.

"Not in front of me," she said. "I'll get embarrassed."

"You think so little of me?"

She raised up on her toes and kissed me on the cheek.

"I think more of you than you can imagine," she whispered in my ear.

She left me then, to chase after our English teacher, Mr. Ramirez. Although not number one in our class, Teri had to give a speech as salutatorian. Mr. Ramirez was probably going to help her with it. She said she had not even begun to write it. Like I believed that. As she walked away, I opened the book and read her note.

> Daniel,
> I have a recurring dream about you that I've never told you about. We are sailing through outer space in a ship made of light and you are sitting in the captain's chair and the simple fact that you're there comforts me. Because in this dream I'm scared. We are on an adventure that I know is filled with danger, but in this dream, each time I look at you, I know that you are there to help. And each day that I see you at school, I feel that this is true. You are magical, you have to find a way to share that magic with the rest of us.
>
> I love ya, I really do,
> Teri

I wasn't given a chance to savor the message, to try to figure out what she was really saying, because Shena was walking toward me then. I couldn't help but stare at her as she did so. Those scars—how deep did they have to cut? If I had a million dollars, I would have given it all to the best plastic surgeon in the world if he could fix her even a little.

It was the left side of Shena's face that was the worst. When the battery had exploded, the acid drenched that side, and there had been no water available to wipe it off. Indeed, Jimmy and Gale had made the mistake, while rushing Shena to the hospital, of keeping the wounds covered with a cloth that was lying in the car. In other words, they had kept the acid on the skin and allowed it to do its worst. I had given Jimmy a bad time about such a stupid move, but he had just mumbled something about how they had been in shock.

The left side of Shena's face was not only seriously scarred, the skin had changed color. On the twisted mass of tissue near her left eye, the skin was dark purple. But around the left side of her mouth it was flame red. Her cheek was orange. I didn't understand why, but had heard Jimmy tell someone that her makeup had melted into her flesh.

Shena was permanently blind in her left eye.

She smiled as she approached; it was a sad smile.

"Did Teri sign your book?" she asked as she gave me a quick hug.

"Yeah. She wrote that I'm better in bed than Sal. Think he'll mind?"

Shena tried to hold on to her smile. "Friends should share everything."

"Wow. A liberal chick, I like it. Can I sign your book?"

"Not yet, I'm not ready to sign yours. I have to think up something juicy." She paused. "I heard about what you did this morning."

"Pretty crazy, huh?"

She looked away and spoke quietly. "I wish I had your guts."

I was careful. "What would you do?"

She glanced at me. "You don't want to know."

"Shena . . ." I began.

She shrugged. "Don't say it. I know you mean well." Again she paused. "Did Jimmy try to shoot the pier today?"

"No. He's not insane."

"Sure. He has a lot to live for." She changed the subject, thank God. "Are you going to ask Gale out today?"

"Going to try." Big pause. "Do you think she'll say yes?"

"I've been telling you forever that I can scope her out for you. But you don't want me to."

"I actually do want you to, but I think I'd be a chicken if I did."

Shena nodded, studied me with her good eye. "I think she likes you. If she doesn't, she's a fool."

"It's amazing how many pretty girls in this school are fools."

Shena gave me a real smile, and it was nice to see. She leaned over and kissed me on the cheek— hopefully it was to be a day filled with kisses. Everyone was happy it was the last day of school but sad as well. Shena had three pictures in the yearbook, all of her before her accident. She had been the prettiest girl in the school.

"I love you," she said with feeling.

I was touched. "You have a lot of love inside you."

She drew back and shook her head. Shook away the smile.

"There's nothing left inside me," she said.

That sort of killed the conversation, to put it mildly. We chatted a minute more, but I could tell she had slipped back into that place filled with tall mirrors that never vanished, even when the lights went out. Even in the night, I was sure, she would awaken to feel her face.

First period was calling, the bell was ringing. Surfing never made me late to Mr. Ramirez's English class because I loved it. The subject matter was a mere formality. We read books and stuff, but mainly we explored what mattered to us, whether it was music, painting, studying, or even relationships. Ramirez was totally loose—anything was cool, as long as you did it with passion. Still, he favored books above all else, and of course I did as well. Ramirez had us write daily in a journal, which only he read. I often wrote him excerpts from my stories, which he loved. It was Ramirez who gave me confidence in my writing. He told everyone who would listen that I was going to be on *The New York Times* bestseller list within five years of graduating.

I had also written him about my unrequited love for Gale.

He called me aside ten minutes into class. Nothing was happening, anyway, other than our partying. We went outside and sat under a tree. He had his acoustic guitar, I swore it was going to get him fired. The other teachers weren't crazy about his unorthodox teaching style.

He, too, had heard about me shooting the pier. I swear Jimmy must have taken out an ad announcing the fact. Ramirez wanted to know what had possessed me.

"I just did it. It was something I wanted to do since I started surfing."

"But Sal said the wave was close to twenty feet. That near the pier, you could have got killed."

"The wave will reach forty feet by the end of the

day. Anyway, I don't plan on doing it again soon, if that's what you're worried about."

Ramirez was short and stocky, with intense dark eyes. I wouldn't say he was handsome, but half the girls in school were in love with him anyway. He was only twenty-eight but seemed older because he appeared so wise. He flashed a rare smile at my remark.

"I was just wondering about your motivation."

I laughed. "I'm not suicidal."

He acted relieved, but it was only an act. "Are you going to ask out Gale today?"

I was feeling the pressure. "Everyone keeps asking. I wish she'd ask me." I paused. "Does she ever mention me in her journals?"

"That's not fair." He changed the subject. "Some of the teachers are going to Disneyland tonight with you kids. I'm bringing my family. My wife Sally wants to meet you. I've let her read your stories, I hope you don't mind."

"I don't mind *if* she liked them. That's great. I'd like to meet your family."

He patted me on the arm and held my eye. "It's been nice having you in my class. You're going to do something important for the world, Daniel, I know it."

I didn't know what to say. Something important? Important was not always good. Hitler had been important. So was the hydrogen bomb. The compliment disturbed me. Now, looking back, I think it was an omen.

CHAPTER

4

Gale wasn't in history and I feared that she had skipped the last day. But I caught sight of her at lunch, eating by herself under a tree. Gale often brought her lunch from home and ate in solitude, which I naturally thought was sexy of her. She had many friends, yet no boyfriend.

Gale was a quiet beauty. Her hair was the color of fading sunshine, her lips as sweet as fresh strawberries. Well, in reality she had blondish brown hair and she did in fact have nice lips. I don't know, maybe she wasn't beautiful, I was the wrong one to ask. Her demeanor was gentle, that was for sure, and she had lovely green eyes. Her body I unfortunately didn't know much about, except that it looked nice from a distance. Yet I knew for a fact that she had wonderful skin. I had touched her hand once, when she wasn't looking.

I hyperventilated for five minutes and said a few prayers to the Virgin Mary and a couple of lesser known deities before I walked up to her. She shielded her eyes from the sun as I approached. I liked that. I had my yearbook in hand, an excuse in case all else failed. She had on baggy white shorts and a red top. Her legs were lightly tanned, totally acceptable. My yearbook had developed a case of the jitters; I had to hold it down with both hands.

"I'm sorry, I can't see who you are," she said in her sweet Gale voice.

"It's Mel Gibson. Daniel, I mean, it's me."

She patted the grass beside her. "Sit down and get out of the glare. It's giving me a headache."

I sat beside her; the ground felt firm and unshakable. I forced a casual smile that felt like a painful grimace. She was chewing on an orange and looking at me as if I were a nice guy, a nice, *friendly* guy, but not someone she'd want to take her clothes off with and make passionate love to. It wasn't a smart idea to think of her naked, being so close to her. The image did nothing to loosen my tongue. I kept right on smiling as if I had tiny nails drilled into the corners of my brain. Thankfully she was enjoying her orange. She nodded at my yearbook.

"I haven't picked mine up yet," she said.

"That's terrible," I said. Perhaps I said it with too much passion, because she raised a quizzical eyebrow.

"I'm going to get it in a few minutes," she said.

"OK."

"Did you go to class today?"

"History, yeah."

"What did we do?" she asked.

"Nothing."

"I didn't miss anything?"

"No."

"That's good," she said.

"Yeah."

She was almost done with her orange, the pressure was intense now. I knew I had to say something witty soon or else risk a lifetime of loneliness. Ordinarily I'm a pretty funny guy, but just looking at her shorted the left hemisphere of my brain. I wasn't sure if I was relieved or not when she smiled—she may have been laughing at me.

"What are you doing, Daniel?" she asked, when I didn't say anything.

I blinked. "Nothing. I'm just tired."

She nodded. "I heard you were up early surfing."

Gale had heard something about me and remembered the fact? Had stored the details away in her adorable little head? I was stunned, really, it was almost as if she had told me she loved me. I'm an easy-to-please kind of guy, and her comment gave me a mountain of confidence.

"Sal and Jimmy and I went to Huntington Beach early," I said. "The surf was up."

She gave me a serious look. "I heard about your heroics."

"Who told you?"

"A dozen people." She paused. "You must have been out of your mind."

Over you. I shrugged. "Sometimes I feel a little wild."

She liked that. "How come you never talked to me all year?"

Shrugs are safe. "I don't know, I guess I didn't want to bother you."

She finished the last of her orange and wiped her hands on the grass.

"I thought you didn't like me," she said. "I thought you thought I was stuck up."

I shook my head violently. "Not at all, you're not the least bit stuck up. You're—you're nice."

"You don't even know me."

"Well, I heard you're nice, from kids who do know you."

"Have you been asking about me?"

"No." I felt brave, the tube was opening, the sun was visible. "Yes."

"Why?"

"Because I just—well, I just was wondering is all. What you were like."

She mocked me, for fun. "You never talked to me in four years. How do I know *you're* not stuck up?"

I managed a smile that didn't look like something stitched on.

"Except for you, everyone in our class thinks I'm totally cool. If not for my lousy grades, I would be giving the valedictorian speech today."

"Your lousy clothes are also a problem," she said bluntly.

That took me aback. "What's wrong with my clothes?"

"They look secondhand."

The ones I was wearing were—my family didn't have a lot of money. "I'm not interested in such superficial stuff."

"Bullshit. You need a new haircut as well. You look like your father cuts your hair."

I looked her in the eye; it was make it or break it

time. "My father does cut my hair. But if you don't like it, you're more than welcome to cut it next time."

Gale considered, her green eyes large. Her skin was flushed with blood. She looked so alive right then, as if she had just been born.

"I could get into that," she said, and reached over and ran her hand through my hair. "Where do you live, Danny?"

She could call me Danny if she wanted, there was nothing wrong with the name. My mother's bingo partners called me Danny. Her fingers seemed to caress every erogenous zone in my body with that one quick pass.

"On Lucinda," I said. "You know where it is?"

"Yeah." A pause, she took her hand back. "Do you know where I live?"

I did, as a matter of fact, nice place to drive by late at night and dream about.

"No," I said.

"I live on Birch, near the fire station."

"Oh. I know where that is. Nice street."

She dug a sandwich out of her bag. "Do you like tuna fish?"

"Yeah." I hated it.

"I hate it." She offered me her sandwich. "Do you want it?"

"I just ate."

"Lunch just started. When did you eat?"

"In history class. If you had been there, instead of ditching, you would have seen."

She was amused. "You know what I like about you, Danny?"

"What?" Revelation time, the sky could open.

"You are so full of it."

I had hoped for better. "You know what I like about you?"

"Yeah." She was quick.

I frowned. "What?"

"My ass."

I struggled. "Why do you say that?"

She was cocky. "I caught you looking at it once."

I was the apple she had yet to take from her bag. I don't know how I spoke.

"Well, you do have a nice ass."

She was interested. "Do you like anything else about me?"

I managed to stay cool. "Your breasts."

Sly smile from Goddess Gale. "You can only imagine."

From terror to boldness. "I have, believe me."

She hit me; I loved being beaten by her. "Don't give me that crap that you've been dreaming about me for four years. I won't believe you."

It was going pretty well, I realized. I tried to sound sincere.

"That's true, you're not an obsession or anything like that. But I have wanted to get to know you better."

"Then why didn't you just talk to me?"

I shrugged. "Because you're pretty and popular and I'm just a nerd with a large brain and small muscles."

She stared at me, all innocence. "I thought you were going to say that you had a large something else. That you would try to impress me, you know."

She was a smooth operator, she was one step ahead of me.

"I am trying to impress you," I said.

She seemed genuinely puzzled. "Why?"

I don't know where the words came from. God or the devil.

"Because I like your ass," I said.

She laughed. "I am not my ass, at least I hope not. Don't you like me as a person?"

So cool, way. "No."

She threw her orange peels at me. "Then I'm not going to cut your hair, Danny Boy."

I absorbed her punishment. I spoke quietly.

"Would you go out with me?" I asked.

She softened. She was surprised. "You want to go out with me?"

"Yes."

Very soft. "Why?"

"Because I like you. A lot, actually."

She considered. "I like you."

I swallowed. "Really?"

"Yeah. I was going to write my phone number in your yearbook. I was hoping you might call me this summer."

These were truly amazing sentences. "No."

She nodded solemnly. "Yeah. You want to go to Disneyland together tonight?"

I had to lower my head, I was overcome.

"Yeah, sure, Gale. I think that would be fun."

Her words were a kiss. "I think so, too, Daniel."

CHAPTER

5

After my last class, I floated home, I didn't need a ride. Really, I walked home a foot off the ground, all two miles. I needed the time to be alone, to savor the moment. I had never felt so happy, nothing in my life had even come close to the high I was experiencing. Before saying goodbye to me, Gale had asked if she could sit next to me during the graduation ceremony, which was strictly against the rules. We were supposed to sit in alphabetical order. But I told her no problem, I could receive someone else's diploma, they were all the same to me. Life was an amazing and miraculous creation of God's love. I mean, I was having a great day. Gale Schrater liked me!

And on the way home I passed a used bookstore.

Touched Books—I had been in the place many times. I read as much as I wrote, and used books were cheaper than those at Barnes & Noble or library fines. Sometimes I was able to buy a box of assorted titles for ten bucks. Lately I had been reading a lot of fantasy and murder mysteries. I was a big J.R.R.

Tolkien and Elmore Leonard fan. I had also developed a fascination with the occult and New Age books. Still thinking of Gale—her face not her ass—I wandered into the store.

The owner was Mr. Barnes, sixty going on ninety. He drank a bottle of Maalox for an after-lunch snack. He had lines on his face as deep as trenches. His glasses were magnifying reading glasses. Each time he greeted me I felt like a fish in a bowl inside his brain. He nodded at me as I came in before going back to his crossword puzzle. He had a dictionary for a head, but I liked him just the same.

I went straight to the New Age section and without looking picked up a book entitled *The Magnetic Reality*. There was a magnet on the cover, streams of colored force lines radiated from pole to pole, red and black etchings of unseen powers. There was also a huge glass eye, poorly drawn, which appeared to be on the verge of shattering. I had never seen the book before. I bought it without glancing at the inside, gave Mr. Barnes a wrinkled dollar, and left the store.

I had never done that before.

My house was empty. Both my parents worked full time, my mother as a nanny for rich snobs, my father at a local warehouse. We didn't have a lot, but my mom and dad were fine people, honest and unpretentious. They both planned to attend my graduation ceremony, which was scheduled for six sharp. My mother was very proud of me. My dad never said anything, but I think he thought I was OK. I hoped they hadn't bothered to get me a present; I hated it when they spent money on me that they didn't have. I really did wear secondhand clothes.

Inside my bedroom, under a poster of Hemingway and a blowup of the cover of *Fahrenheit 451,* I plopped down on my bed and opened my new book. The first chapter explained how a magnet could be used to obtain readings on practically any subject. All one had to do was tie it to the end of a string and ask yes or no questions. If the answer was yes, it would swing one way, either clockwise, counterclockwise, or from side to side. If the answer was no it would do the opposite of whatever the yes response was. To establish what was the right direction, it was necessary to ask questions one definitely knew to have yes answers. It all sounded pretty simple and totally unbelievable.

Still, I had a small magnet in my desk drawer. I took it out and tied a short string to one end—as stipulated, the south pole. Then I held it above a blank piece of paper on my desk and tried to steady my hand.

"Am I a male?" I asked.

There was a long pause. But slowly, very slowly, it began to swing in a clockwise direction—from my perspective directly above it. For a moment I was sure I must be making it swing, but it seemed to have a life of its own.

"Am I female?" I asked.

It swung counterclockwise.

"Wow," I mumbled.

Of course I knew about the subconscious, how I could be moving it without realizing it. In fact, that was the only explanation. Certainly the magnet itself didn't understand my questions. I set my new toy down and read more of the book. The author talked about how the magnet allowed one to tap into layers of the mind ordinarily blocked. But then he took it a step further and spoke of unlocking the mystery of Universal Consciousness. I didn't understand what that was, except it sounded cool. Gale was going out with me, and now I was able to talk to the universe, all in the same day.

I grabbed the magnet again.

"Do I love Gale?" I asked.

Yes. It swung clockwise. Smart magnet.

"Does Gale love me?"

Sort of. It went clockwise but without enthusiasm. I was annoyed.

"Is someone answering these questions besides me?"

Yes and *no.* It swung clockwise, then counterclockwise. I didn't understand the response. It seemed it should be one way or the other.

"Are you a human being?" I asked.

Yes and *no.* The *no* was stronger.

"Are you more than my subconscious?"

Yes.

"Are you more than me but connected to me?"

Yes. Very strong.

"Are you a spirit?"

Sort of.

"Are you from this planet?"

No.

"Do you like talking to me?"

37

Yes.

"Are you friendly to me?"

Yes.

"Are you an extraterrestrial?"

Yes. Very strong.

"Cool," I whispered.

Yes.

"Do you like this method of communication?"

No.

"Is it too limiting?"

Yes.

"Can we communicate another way?"

Yes.

"Can you tell me how?"

Yes.

"How? I mean, I have to make suggestions?"

Yes.

"Can I talk to you on a Ouija board?"

Yes and *no.*

"Can I use the magnet in another way to communicate with you?"

Yes.

I couldn't think of another way.

"Is it important we communicate?"

Yes.

"Are you real?"

Yes.

"Could I be deluding myself?"

Yes.

That last answer made me pause. Once again, it seemed contradictory. But it did give me an idea of another method of communication, which was related to the Ouija board, but also different.

"Can I use the magnet to seek out letters rather than your just responding yes or no?"

Yes.

"If I get a large piece of paper, and print out each letter of the alphabet, can I use the magnet to seek out each letter you want?"

Sort of.

My question had been fuzzy.

"Will *you* seek out the appropriate letters you need to spell certain words?"

Yes. Very strong.

"The magnet will only react when it comes over the correct letter?"

Yes.

"Should I do this now?"

Yes.

I set the magnet down and went to my father's den, where he was fond of painting and drawing in the evening. He was a fan of fine paper, and collected it, his only indulgence. He wouldn't mind if I stole a piece, he was always trying to teach me to draw. But I had the hand-mind coordination of a surfer bum; I could only manage happy faces with halos.

I used a black marker pen to carefully print out the letters of the alphabet and arrange them in three neat rows. I also put in periods and commas. By now I was getting excited, and not just because the magnet was swinging. There was a strange energy prickling at the back of my head and the base of my spine. I could have been imagining it, but I didn't think so. The charge was the same as that generated by a coming storm, only much stronger and obviously much more localized.

It felt as if someone were really there.

Something. An energy being.

I returned to my bedroom and picked up my magnet. The sheet I placed directly in front of my crossed legs. Dangling the magnet by the string, I hung it over the alphabet, moving slowly through the letters, starting from *A*. It reacted sharply when it came to *H*, spinning clockwise.

"You want an *H?*" I asked.

Yes.

I wrote down *H* and started again from *A*. When I reached *I* it reacted.

"Hi?" I asked.

Yes.

"You are saying hi to me?"

Yes.

"Hi there," I said. "Should I continue?"

Yes.

"Should I ask questions first?"

Yes.

"Who are you?"

The answer was long and slow in coming. But finally I had it and my heart was pounding. I capitalized what words I thought appropriate. The magnet did make use of my comma and period.

You may call me Mentor. I am you and I am not you. I am a higher aspect of you. I reside in what you would call a subtle body on a world six hundred and forty-two light-years from you. This world is called Ortee. We are advanced beyond the inhabitants of your planet, both materially and spiritually. Eighteen of your years ago, a portion of my consciousness left here and incarnated on your planet. That portion you call the soul.

"You've got to be kidding me," I blurted out.

I had to work the magnet to get the answer.

I am serious, Daniel. I contact you at this time to make you and your friends aware of your mission.

"Which friends?"

You know the ones, the six of you.

"You mean Jimmy? Sal? Teri? Shena?"

And Gale.

"I hardly know Gale."

But she is one of the six.

I was giddy. Cool, I knew her from the stars. Not that I really believed what was being spelled out, not in any absolute sense.

"Then she does love me?"

It is a mystery.

"What is our mission?"

To help humanity.

"Why us?"

All are born to help. But being from a higher world, you are especially qualified.

"What are our special qualifications?"

When you all awake to your true identity, they will manifest.

"How do we awaken ourselves?"

As a group. I will direct you.

"When?"

Soon.

"Will the others believe in you?"

Not at first. But they know me. I am their true friend.

41

"But exactly how will you awaken us?"

When you are together, I will speak through you. There is a great power in your group consciousness. We will go to an isolated place.

Something odd occurred to me.

"Was Teri's dream accurate?"

There was truth in it. I placed the dream in her mind, many times.

"Did I get the idea for my story from you?"

You are writing your own story.

"We are the Star Group?"

Yes.

"When you say you will speak through me, will it be like all this New Age channeling?"

No. Channeling is dangerous. We communicate through a high form of telepathy. You will be aware at all times of who you are and what you are saying.

"Why is channeling dangerous?"

It produces distorted information. It also weakens mind-body coordination.

"Is there a possibility of distortion with you?"

Yes.

"Why?"

If you have a deep desire, it can distort what information I am able to bring through you.

"Do I have such deep desires?"

Yes.

"What are they?"

Your infatuation with Gale for one. But there are others. Be alert to them.

"OK." I paused. "But is there any danger in doing this thing you want?"

Any knowledge can be used for constructive or destructive purposes. There is no danger in acting as my receiver. But the powers we intend to awaken in your group can be misused.

"How can I be here on Earth and on your planet as well?"

Time is an illusion. Also, the soul is multidimensional.

"But are we exactly the same person?"

It is complicated. We are aspects of the same being.

"This method of communicating is tiring. My hands are exhausted. When will you be able to speak through me?"

Soon.

"Can you be more specific?"

No. I do not wish to destroy your innocence.

"I would like proof that you exist. Can you give me such proof?"

In time.

"Which is only an illusion?"

It is an illusion that is real for you.

"How long have you been monitoring our group?"

Since you were born.

"Did you help me shoot the pier this morning?"

No.

"Could I have died trying?"

Yes.

"Was it a foolish thing to do?"

Very.

Our little talk had taken over an hour. I had to get ready for graduation. Plus my hands really were hurting, and the muscles had actually begun to twitch. Still, it was hard to quit. I liked Mentor. Besides his strange knowledge, he had a subtle sense of humor.

"I have to go now. When should we talk again?"

Tomorrow night. Have fun at Disneyland.

"Should I try to kiss Gale?"

You suffer many illusions.

I laughed. "I'm sure I do."

Shena is in a bad space. Care for her.

I lost my laugh. The energy had changed, become somehow heavier.

"Is there a danger to our group because of what happened to Shena?"

Mentor seemed to hesitate. For a minute nothing would spell out. Then he merely repeated himself.

Care for her.

"I will do my best," I said as I set the magnet down. "Bye."

I assumed my higher self said goodbye.

Now the odd thing was that the whole communication did not freak me out. It was odd how calm I felt about it, as if I had known Mentor all my life. If what he had said was true, maybe I had. I didn't accept his explanation, even his existence, but I did not dismiss it, either. All I knew was that I wanted to talk to him some more as soon as I could. As soon as my hands felt up to it. I couldn't imagine actually talking *for* him, that was too far out.

Anyway, I was a teenager and it was time for my all-night party. Mentor was abstract, Gale was real, and soon she would be sitting beside me. I had to look my best. Heading for the bathroom, I grabbed a pair of scissors and a hand mirror and my mother's best shampoo. I did have a new shirt and pair of pants set out for the big night.

But I didn't have a car, I just remembered.

I jumped out of my shower, totally naked, and called Jimmy.

"Hello?"

"Jimmy. She said yes."

I heard him grin. "Did you ask her to marry you?"

"No. But we're going to Disneyland together tonight. Can I borrow your car?"

No doubt I was putting him out, way out. But he didn't hesitate.

"Sure. I'll call Sal. I can go with him and Teri."

"What about Shena?"

He sighed. "I don't know about Shena."

"Is she going to the ceremony?"

"I don't know." He changed the subject. "The principal asked me to give a short speech after Teri's and Susan Meyer's."

Susan Meyer was our valedictorian, and the most boring person on the face of the Earth. From her pinched expression one would think she was constantly downloading massive files into her tight skull.

"What are you going to talk about?" I asked.

"You and Gale. How it took you four years to ask her out."

"Don't you dare! I'm going to be sitting beside her."

Jimmy laughed. "I think I'll leave you in doubt. That's the price you have to pay for borrowing my car on this night of nights. Do you want me to pick you up?"

"Yeah. My parents are going to meet me there."
Jimmy paused. "I'm proud of you, you know."
"For shooting the pier or for Gale?"
"For having the nerve to borrow my car."
I laughed. "Be here at five-thirty. We can't be late."
"I'll be there," Jimmy promised.

CHAPTER

6

The graduation ceremony was to be held outside at Whittier College, in the stadium. Whittier College's only claim to fame was that it had been the alma mater of President Nixon. Otherwise it was a pretty boring place, as was the rest of Whittier, which adjoined La Mirada, another boring place. No wonder Mentor wanted to take us elsewhere to awaken our souls. The local vibe was not inspiring.

We had a glorious evening, clear skies and warm temperatures. Our school colors were blue and gold. I was not a knockout student but had earned enough A's and B's to get a gold tassel. Jimmy and I kidded each other in the college parking lot as we threw on our gowns.

"We look like priests," he said.

I tried on my hat or cap or whatever it was called. "We should be allowed to keep these gowns. They cost us twenty bucks."

"And when are you going to wear a graduation gown again?"

47

He had a point. "I'm a nostalgic kind of guy."

"If things go well with Gale tonight you might be dreaming of tonight for the rest of your life." He grinned. "Do you have condoms?"

"Get out of here! I don't just want her for her body."

"But you do want her body?"

"Sure. But she's not going to sleep with me on the first date."

"She might; it's a special night. She might want to try to make it more special."

"You're crude."

"I'm a realist. Do you want condoms or not? I have an extra pack in my glove compartment." He added quietly, "I haven't used them lately."

I looked around at the people pouring into the stadium.

"We have to take good care of Shena," I said.

Jimmy looked at me strangely. "That's what I've been trying to do this last six months."

"Jimmy? Can I ask you a personal question?"

"Yeah."

"Was it your fault?"

He stopped. "I don't think so."

"What happened exactly?"

He shook his head and locked up the car. "I don't want to talk about it, not tonight." He added, "Tonight is supposed to be fun."

I nodded as he handed me his keys. "Sorry. I just worry about you two."

He was not offended, that was the great thing about Jimmy. He could let the little things go. Unfortunately, he was mortal and could not drop the big things.

But Jimmy asked me a weird question as we walked toward the stadium.

"What did you do this afternoon?"

"What do you mean?" I asked.

He studied me. "You look like you were up to something."

I shrugged. "I don't know what you're talking about."

Inside, the stadium was crowded. Family members and friends were in the stands; our class sat on folding chairs on the football field, around a raised stage. The latter was decorated with flowers, posh chairs, and a huge banner. Jimmy left me for the stage and the other celebrities. Naturally I was searching everywhere for Gale, but I found Sal and Teri first. It did my heart good to see them standing hand in hand. Sal waved me over; he somehow looked more dignified than the rest of us in his blue gown. He shook my hand as I approached, like I had just won an Olympic gold medal.

"I heard you popped the question and she said yes," he said. "Good job."

"I paid her to say yes," Teri said. She giggled when she saw my face fall. "Look at our sensitive boy. No, Daniel, I'm just teasing you."

I was still looking. "Have you seen her?"

"Yeah, Gale's around." Sal lowered his voice. "But Shena told me she's not coming. This evening or tonight."

The news stung. "When did you talk to her?"

"I called her an hour ago. I offered to pick her up, but she said no. She sounded horrible."

"I want to visit her before we go to Disneyland," Teri said. "I can't stand the thought of her sitting home alone tonight. I'll stay with her if I have to."

I appreciated Teri's willingness to sacrifice.

"This is turning out to be a complicated day," I muttered.

Sal shook his head. "It's a big bad world out there."

Teri stared at him with such repressed emotion, it made my heart ache.

"It doesn't have to be so bad," she said. "We make our own choices."

Sal looked away. "A lot of choices are made for us."

I didn't want the conversation to sink down.

"Hey, let's sit down," I said. "The teachers are all pointing at the chairs. I think they want to get started."

The three of us ignored our seating assignments and sat together in the rear. This was brave of Teri since she was supposed to speak. Sal told her to get up there, but she just shook her head and gripped his hand.

Gale joined us two minutes later.

She looked much better than Sal in her gown. She looked, in fact, like everything I had ever dreamed of. Her blond bangs peeked out from beneath her cap and her green eyes sparkled with excitement. She still looked flushed, as she had that afternoon, with life and excitement. I hoped I played a small part in her enthusiasm.

"We're going to have to step over people when they call our names," she said.

"I don't care if you don't care," I said.

"I certainly don't care." She studied me. "I think long blue gowns suit you."

"Because they cover everything up?"

"That's it." Gale looked over at Teri. "What's your speech about?"

Teri glanced at Sal. "Making commitments."

Gale was interested. "In relationships? School? Work?"

Teri let go of Sal's hand and crossed her arms over her chest.

"All of the above," she said.

"Just don't mention me in your speech," Sal muttered.

"No problem," Teri said.

Gale peeked under my cap. "Did you cut your hair?"

I shrugged. "Just a little."

"But I wanted to cut it. You promised me."

I pushed my cap back down. "When you see it later you'll be relieved to know it needs a lot more attention."

"I heard your car's not working," Gale said.

"Where did you hear that?" I asked.

"I just spoke to your parents."

"*What?*" I hadn't been able to find them myself.

Gale grinned. "They're neat. I met them in the parking lot. They told me a lot about you and made you sound like a good catch. But I don't know, I'm kind of suspicious that they're prejudiced."

"What did they say exactly?"

"That you've been pining away for me for years."

I acted bored. "They're confusing you with somebody else."

She poked me. I got the feeling she liked to touch. "What's her name?"

"*Their* names. Not one of them is called Gale."

She acted offended. "Hey, you want to take me to Disneyland or not?"

I nodded. "I do. Don't worry, I got Jimmy's car."

Gale's face darkened. "I feel terrible Shena's not here."

"It's not your fault."

Gale shook her head. "I was there that night, remember? It was my fault as much as anybody's." She paused. "I think Shena hates me, too."

"Shena doesn't hate anyone."

Gale stared at the stage. "I wouldn't be so sure about that."

Finally the ceremony got under way. We pledged our allegiances to the flag and sang the national anthem. The principal introduced our class—we all shouted and waved our caps—and then the class president said a few boring words. Then I got the shock of my life. He called Gale up to sing a song. She stood nonchalantly.

"Did you know you had to sing?" I gasped.

"Yeah." She smiled. "You didn't know I could, did you?"

"No. What else can you do?"

She giggled. "You should be so lucky to know."

Gale walked casually onto the stage and nodded to

another music student at the piano. The crowd applauded lightly as she stepped behind the microphone and then settled down. I noticed Teri smiling slyly. Gale began to sway slightly, even before she burst into song. The piano suddenly exploded in familiar chords. Elton John—"Crocodile Rock."

"I remember when rock was young! Me and Suzy had so much fun!"

Our entire graduating class jumped up and started dancing. Obviously, with the song so near the beginning, the organizing committee hadn't planned on Gale's bringing down the house. But it was her moment and she seized it. By the time she was finished singing—she added a few verses—we were all soaked with sweat. Our families and friends didn't mind—they responded enthusiastically. Gale laughed and bowed and returned to her seat. I loved how everyone watched when she sat down beside me. She couldn't stop laughing.

"This must be how you felt when you shot the pier," she said.

"Did you ask if you could sing that?" I asked.

"Yeah. McManus said no!"

Sal reached over and patted her on the back.

"For a white girl, you sure do have soul," he said.

Gale was still giggling. "I take that as the highest compliment. I'll pass it on to Elton John, in fact."

Susan Meyer, our valedictorian, had to follow Gale, which was not easy. She "brilliantly" chose to talk about the economy, and the role young people would play in it. Everyone started talking. But I did manage to keep a straight face and remain quiet.

Teri was next. Standing behind the microphone, she pulled her speech out of her pocket and seemed to study it. But then she folded it up and put it back, her expression serious.

"I'm sure the last thing you all want to hear is another speech from an uninformed adolescent. I don't know anything about the economy or what our society needs to survive. I don't know much about the environment, either. I just hope we don't mess up this world so bad that it can't be fixed. I mean, I'm just getting out of high school. But what I do know is that I love a lot of people here." She took in the whole audience for a long moment, and when she finally spoke her voice cracked. "And I'm going to miss them, miss their love. Thank you."

We were all stunned by the brevity of her speech, but then we burst out in applause. In seconds Teri had blown away Susan Meyer's speech. When she returned to her seat, Sal gave her a kiss.

Jimmy swaggered up to the mike next.

From his walk, I should have known I was in trouble.

"Hi," he said. "My name is James Yearn and my speech is short as well. In fact, I don't have a speech. But I do want to share something that happened to my friends and me today. Sal Barry and Daniel Stevens and I went surfing this morning, and as you might have heard, the waves are bigger than they've been in twenty years. Anyway, we were out on our boards when the biggest wave of the day rolled in. It must have been twenty-five feet. It literally touched the bottom of the pier. Now Daniel had never shot the pier before, but something came over him right then. It was like he was possessed. He paddled into that wave and took off, standing up, his board aimed right at the pier. Sal and I thought he was a goner. The wave swept right over him, and we thought we'd soon be searching for his body. But what we didn't know was that Daniel had entered the greatest of all tubes. He had attained the highest state of nirvana that a surfer can reach. Only when he emerged on the other side of the pier did we know that by the grace of God he had survived and returned to us."

Jimmy paused and smiled. "Now you probably want to know what this has to do with anything. Honestly . . . I don't have the slightest idea. It's just that it was so cool, such an impossible feat, and it was done by someone in our class. I just needed to share it with you. Also, I'd like to ask Daniel to stand and take a bow. Please, ladies and gentlemen, give him a big hand for either being the bravest guy in the world or the dumbest!"

I sat there petrified. The audience started to clap.

Gale poked me. "Get up!"

"No," I mumbled. The audience began to stand.

Gale pinched me and hissed. "Coward!"

Calm descended from above. Perhaps Mentor came to my rescue. I looked at Gale and smiled. "One thing you should know about me, I'm not a coward."

When I stood and waved, the audience exploded in cheers.

My class did likewise. Great final note to high school.

I was mad at Jimmy but grateful, too.

Jimmy called for our class to throw our caps in the air.

Five hundred blue birds flew for the sky.

I caught Gale's as it fell and returned it to her.

She kissed me on the lips and laughed.

"But you're not as brave as I am," she said.

CHAPTER

7

Disneyland was cool, at least at the start. First off, the place was reserved *only* for graduating high school seniors and a few teachers that night, which I only learned when we got there. There weren't two dozen senior classes celebrating but several hundred. It was fun to walk around and see so many people all the same age. It was a warm clear night, with a half moon hanging in the sky. As Gale and I strolled up Main Street, we couldn't stop smiling.

"We're going to have a blast," she said. "And I want you to spend money on me. I want a Minnie Mouse T-shirt and a Minnie Mouse baseball cap."

"I'm lucky my parents gave me money for graduation," I said. "You sound like an expensive chick."

"I am an expensive chick." She paused. "How much did they give you?"

"A hundred dollars."

She waved her hand. "That's not much."

"For my parents it is," I said.

She poked me again. "I was just teasing. I told you, I adore your parents."

"Thanks. I wish I'd met yours."

Gale was watching me. "They weren't there." She didn't explain and I didn't ask.

"Really? That's too bad."

"Did you know I'm adopted?"

"No."

"I've never met my real parents." She paused and her voice faltered. "Maybe they would have come if they'd known."

I was hesitant to probe. I squeezed her arm.

We met Sal, Teri, and Jimmy as planned. They had told us they wanted to stop by Shena's house to try to persuade her to come. Then we'd all meet in front of the Matterhorn. When we gathered, I asked about Shena. Teri shook her head.

"There was no talking to that girl," she said.

Jimmy wanted to change the subject. He always did when it was about Shena. He asked how I felt about his speech. I hadn't had a chance to tell him. I shook my head.

"If I wasn't in such a great mood tonight," I said, "I'd have killed you."

"That means you owe your life to me," Gale told Jimmy. "I put him in the good mood."

"And how exactly did you do that?" Sal asked, smoking a cigarette.

Gale grinned. "I have my ways."

The others howled, and I tried not to blush. But, of course, I failed.

We got in line for Magic Mountain. Teri insisted on riding before we ate anything—she said she didn't want to throw up on us. The line was long, but I didn't mind because Gale stood close the whole time. Then, when we were inside the dark roller coaster and going down fast, she instinctively put an arm around my waist. I liked to think it was instinct, that she already trusted me.

We hung out in Tomorrowland for a while and then made our way over to It's a Small World. It was the one ride I couldn't stand, but Teri and Gale seemed excited about it so I acted excited, too. Yet it was odd: in the middle of the ride, with all the smiling idiot puppets singing their repetitious song, I suddenly felt the same energy in my head and spine as I had when I communicated with Mentor. What was even more odd was that I had forgotten all about him since graduation. Maybe he was trying to tell me that our world really was small. Gale looked at me as the energy touched me.

"Are you all right?" she asked.

I blinked. "Yes, I'm fine. Why do you ask?"

"Your eyes are dilated."

"It's from staring at you."

She raised an eyebrow. "The last four years?"

"That must be it."

I noticed one of the seven dwarfs start to follow us after we got off the ride, but paid it no heed. I mean, I wasn't into dwarfs.

Next we went to eat at some fast-food joint. But because it was Disneyland, it cost as much as a fine restaurant. I was really glad my parents had given me money, my earlier vow notwithstanding. It was nice to be able to pay for Gale's food.

We met Mr. Ramirez and his family at the hamburger joint. His wife was so pretty that I could see how he stayed away from all the hot girls at school. His two kids, a boy and a girl, were sweet, their eyes sparkling with the night lights and excitement. Mr. Ramirez congratulated Teri on her short but emotional speech.

"I was touched," he said.

"What about my speech?" Jimmy asked. He was asking everyone.

Ramirez shook his head. "It was unique. I think it must have taken as much guts to make a fool of yourself as it did for Daniel to shoot the pier."

Jimmy nodded. "That was exactly why I did it. To praise Daniel and show him up at the same time."

I noticed that the dwarf had followed us to the restaurant. I was going to point him out and ask the others which one he was, but he turned away when I looked at him. Again, I didn't give it much thought.

We headed for Pirates of the Caribbean next. Along the way we teamed up with Judy Farley and Cindy Converse. Both were cheerleaders and it was Cindy who had inherited Shena's mantle as most beautiful girl in the school. She was an exquisite brunette with long brown hair and thick lips surrounding a sensual mouth. When Cindy saw that Jimmy was alone, she immediately started hitting on him and I was disappointed that Jimmy returned her affections. Jimmy and Sal were slightly drunk, I could smell the alcohol and figured they had put away a few beers in the parking lot. Sal could drink and maintain his dignity, but Jimmy got wild. As Cindy jostled close to him in the Pirates line, Jimmy pinched her side and bumped his head against hers. It looked painful but Cindy seemed to like it.

The two snuggled close in the back row of the ride. But I had other things on my mind—Gale squeezed up close to me as the pirates fought all around us.

"Are you having a good time?" she asked.

"Wonderful. You?"

She pressed closer, staring up at me with her darling green eyes.

"It's special to spend tonight with you," she said.

I chuckled nervously. "We should have done this earlier."

"You should have asked me out before." She paused. "Why didn't you?"

A serious question. I told her the truth.

"I was afraid," I said.

She liked that. "Afraid of little old me?"

"Not anymore."

She leaned over and kissed my cheek. "Good."

When we exited the ride, with Jimmy and Cindy on much closer terms, I noticed that the dwarf was right behind us. I seemed to be the only one who saw him. I brought our roving band to a halt; I mean this dwarf was definitely trailing us. I pointed him out to the others and this time he froze.

"Who is that dwarf?" I asked. "He's been following us half the night."

Teri giggled. "I think it's Dopey."

"No," Sal said. "There was no prejudice against white people in my house while I was growing up so we watched *Snow White* a lot. That's Sleepy."

Jimmy squinted, his arm around Cindy. "I think it's Shorty."

"There's no dwarf named Shorty," I said.

"There should be!" Cindy howled. She was clearly drunk.

I strode over to where the dwarf was standing. Naturally it wore a happy face, but its demeanor was anything but joyful. It lowered its head at my approach.

"Why are you following us?" I demanded.

The voice came out muffled, female. "Welcome to the happiest place on Earth."

"Yeah, sure," I said as the others moved closer. "Who are you?"

"Snow White," the Dwarf said. "The fairest in all the land."

Jimmy lost his stupid smile and let go of Cindy. He should have guessed. I had. "Who are you?" he whispered.

Shena took off her dwarf head; it took her a whole minute. Jimmy aged visibly in that short time. She smiled at us as she shook her hair free, but it was a forced smile. The gang just stared.

"I have a friend who works here," she explained. "She let me borrow her costume. I thought I would surprise you all." She turned to Cindy. "Having fun?"

Cindy was no longer drunk. She edged away from Jimmy.

"I'll catch you guys later," she mumbled.

Cindy left us. Shena strode toward Jimmy and offered him her dwarf head to carry. He took it and seemed unable to look away from its bulbous black eyes. Shena kept her smile in place. She flashed it at all of us, the strained lips, the shaking teeth.

"Why don't Jimmy and I give this costume back to its rightful owner and we can join you guys in a few minutes?" she asked. "Where are you going next?"

We agreed to meet in our usual place, at the Matterhorn, in twenty minutes. Our group was now a lot less carefree. As we walked toward the ride Teri warned us that sparks were going to fly.

"When we're in line I'll talk to her," Gale offered. "I'm not as close to the situation as you guys. It might be better."

"It might be better if we went to Magic Mountain instead," Sal said, naming an amusement park fifty miles away.

"Jimmy shouldn't have been fooling around with Cindy," I said.

Sal shook his head. "Who really knows what goes on between those two?"

We were about to get an insider's view.

The Matterhorn line moved faster than the one at Space Mountain. Jimmy and Shena had barely rejoined us when we were ushered into the bobsleds. But Gale did get a chance to talk to her alone for two minutes, and it seemed to do some good. Shena giggled as she jumped to the head of our group. Each bobsled held six, with our questionable couple in front. As the bobsled slowly inched its way to the top of the Matterhorn, it suddenly stopped. None of us was alarmed, rides halted all the time, and Disneyland had measures in place to protect people in case of equipment failure. Yet we were hanging at a precarious angle, our noses up in the air. And we were carrying volatile cargo.

Jimmy and Shena started to fight.

We didn't want to listen, but we had to.

"I wasn't making a move on her," Jimmy hissed. "I was just being friendly."

"You practically had your hand on her breast!" Shena whispered angrily.

"That's ridiculous! I did not touch her breasts!"

"Not tonight! What about last night? The night before?"

"Shh! We'll talk about this later."

"Later? What later? I won't see you later! You should be grateful, you won't have my ugly face in your face anymore!"

"Shena!"

"I am not Shena! Shena is dead!"

With that Shena squirmed out from under the computer-controlled steel bar that kept us firmly in our seats and jumped onto the side of the mountain, literally. Before Jimmy could stop her she began to climb up the side of the Matterhorn, toward a precipice from which it would be very easy to sky dive into Suicide Land. Jimmy was brave, he went after her, and Sal chased after Jimmy. The scene would have been comical, the three of them swearing and running on the backside of an amusement park ride, but the angles and height had me worried. One slip, intentional or not, and one of them could die. Teri turned to me.

"Do something, Daniel!" she cried.

I fought against the steel bar. It budged slowly. Gale grabbed my arm.

"You're not going anywhere!" she exclaimed. "You can't help them. The park personnel will be here in a minute."

"A minute is a long time," I said.

Gale gripped tighter. "No!"

I released the bar. I shook off Gale's hand and carefully stood. Then I patted Gale on the shoulder. She looked frantic, as did Teri.

"Today's my lucky day," I said. "I'll be all right."

I leaped onto the side of the artificial mountain; it really was steep. The other three had gone around a bend, and I had to climb twenty feet to find them. The scene was not good. Shena was poised at the edge of a cliff, and the guys were pleading for her to come down. There were maybe ten feet between them and her. Apparently she had already threatened to jump.

"This is just a misunderstanding," Jimmy said desperately. "I don't care for Cindy. I only care about you."

Shena shook her head and wept. "I don't care about Cindy! It's me that's the problem! No guy could possibly love me! I'm a freak!"

Jimmy tried to move closer. "You're not a freak. You're a wonderful girl. You have your whole life in front of you. It will be a wonderful life, you just have to get past this time. We can get through it together, I promise you. Please come down before you hurt yourself."

"Stay back!" she screeched. "I'll jump!"

Sal moved in front of Jimmy and caught Shena's eye.

"Shena, listen to me," he said calmly. "Suicide is bullshit. You die and we all feel like hell. But maybe that's what you want. But, think, think real hard, you might go to hell for doing it. Who knows what there really is? No one knows anything for sure in this crazy world. But you might just make your problem a thousand times worse. Now you don't want to do that, not to yourself and not to us. We love you. I know Jimmy does and I know I do. Come down because you love us. I'm begging you, Shena, I really am." He reached out to her. "Come to me, Shena. I'll take care of you, I won't let you fall."

Sal's words were powerful. We were all crying, but I couldn't wipe my tears away without releasing my grip on the mountain. Shena's tears gushed from both her eyes, the good one and the bad. Maybe the water cleared her vision somehow, inside and out. The lines of pain on her ruined face softened and she lowered her head and nodded. Moving slowly, Sal climbed up to her and embraced her. Jimmy joined them a few seconds later, and I managed to make it to them a minute later. I held her as tight as I had ever held anyone in my life. The horror of her brush with death penetrated my soul.

I felt if she had died, we all would have died.

But maybe that would have been for the best.

CHAPTER

8

On the ride home Gale told me her parents were out of the country, which explained why they weren't at graduation.

"Where are they?" I asked.

"In Europe." She glanced over at me. "Don't feel sorry for me, I like to be alone."

"But it must be lonely for you at a time like this."

She touched my leg. "I have you to keep me company."

I teased. "Do you *have* me?"

She let go of my leg and nodded. "Yes."

Her house was much nicer than mine, but it wasn't extravagant. Her driveway was concrete and the hedges were all trimmed. She had a nice wooden front door. As we strode into the place, I noticed the sweet smell of incense. I commented on it, and she pointed out an incense holder above the fireplace.

"I burn it when I practice meditation," she said.

"Really? How do you meditate?"

She considered my question a long time. "I don't

know. It just happens if I sit silently and close my eyes."

"I'm interested in it because I read a lot of esoteric literature."

She nodded as she turned on more lights. I followed her to the rear of the house, and was surprised when she lit up a rectangular pool in the wide backyard with a flick of a switch. Steam slowly rose from the water and I heard the gurgling of pumps and pipes.

"Do you swim much?" I asked.

She stared at me. "Yes. Do you want to swim?"

I blushed, bad habit. "I don't have any trunks."

She came closer, touched my shirt. "We can go skinny dipping."

I stammered. "On our first date?"

She smiled shyly. "I won't look if you don't." She raised up on tiptoe and brushed my lips with hers. She tasted like vanilla ice cream with cherries on top. "But if you look I'll have to look, too."

I was having a minor coronary, but it was OK.

I swallowed. "I'd like to swim with you."

She squeezed my hand and went away. "Take off your clothes and get in the water. I'll be there in a minute."

I did as she asked. I mean, I would have been a fool to argue with her when she was in such an obviously generous mood. The water was delicious; it seemed to warm my heart as well as my skin. There was no question, I felt as if I had died and gone to heaven.

But then I recalled how close Shena had come to death.

The park officials had ordered all of us to leave the park.

It was only a little after midnight. Not late.

Gale was wearing a beach towel when she came out of the house five minutes later. Her dark blond hair seemed longer right then, for some reason, and when she tossed aside the towel before stepping in the water, her eyes flashed with a wonderful light. Once again she appeared to me as the embodiment of all desire, a heart that pulsed with a life I could only hope to draw close to. She was beyond me, I knew it, but I still thanked God that He should allow me to spend even a brief time with her. My fatalistic attitude was as potent as ever. She swam into my arms and kissed me and pressed close so that I could feel the whole of her body. Her lips were so warm.

"Daniel," she said as we kissed and touched.

I needed a dozen hands. "Yes?"

"Do you like me?"

"Yeah. I guess."

Her tongue pressed against mine. There was a pause.

"Do you love me?" she whispered.

"I guess," I mumbled.

She drew back; it was nice to see all of her. Thank God for shallow ends.

"You're not sure?" she asked, and maybe she was hurt.

I pulled her back. "It's always a possibility."

She moved her mouth to my ear.

"I will make you sure," she promised.

* * *

Much later, when we were lying naked in her bed together, her head resting on my contented chest, she asked if I had ever slept with a girl before.

"No," I said. "At least, not that I remember."

She liked that. She got up on her elbows. The light in the room was low, the moon peeking in through lacy curtains. Her skin seemed to glow.

"Would you be upset if I told you that you weren't the first?"

I considered. "You do seem experienced." I hastily added, "That's not necessarily bad."

She studied me. "I won't tell you who it was, but it was somebody at school."

I felt a stab of jealousy. "Tell me."

She played with my hair. "No."

"Why not?"

"I don't screw and tell."

"Is that what we're doing? Screwing?"

She tugged at my hair. "Screwing is not a bad thing. But I'd like us to go somewhere after tonight."

"Where?"

She kissed my chest. "Somewhere special. A realm of magic."

I touched her hair. "You are magic."

"Thank you."

"But you can tell me who it was, I won't get upset."

She ran her nail along my lower lip. "Yes. You will."

"How do you know?"

"It was someone you know."

Not a pleasant thought. "Who?"

"I told you already, I don't tell. It doesn't matter, it's over now."

"But how well do I know this person?"

She looked sad.

"We shouldn't be talking about this. Please?"

"All right." I felt unsettled. "What do you want to talk about?"

Her mood had changed. She sat up and stared at the window, then reached out and pulled the lacy curtains aside. The unfiltered moonlight on her face made her appear ghostlike. A spirit from an alien world.

"Shena scared me tonight," she said softly. "I thought she'd do it."

"What?"

"You know. Die." She paused. "Do you think about death much?"

"Yes." I paused. "I think that's why I'm drawn to esoteric books. But I am beginning to think death is a mystery that can't be solved."

"Shena almost solved it tonight."

"I don't think solving the age-old riddle was her motivation."

Gale stared at me. "Jimmy did tell her to hook up the cables the wrong way. I saw it all. When I turned on my car and gunned the engine, the battery exploded right in her face. It *was* his fault and she has a right to hate him."

I sat up. "Do you hate him?"

Of course I was asking another question.

I was relieved when she shook her head. "I don't hate anyone."

"Why didn't you wash the acid off her face immediately?" I asked.

71

"We had no water."

"But why didn't you just wipe it off?"

Gale grimaced. "I wanted to, but she was crying so hard. I was afraid of wiping off her skin." She paused. "But I should have done something. Do you know a day doesn't go by that I don't think of that night? Sometimes, lying here in the dark, it's *all* I can think of. Pretty sick, huh?"

"No. It means you're compassionate."

"Am I? When she was screaming in pain, I kept thinking that I was glad it was her who had been standing next to the battery and not me. Does that make me cool?"

"It was an accident. There was nothing you could do."

She studied me. "But you were questioning me. I don't know if you really believe there was nothing I could do."

"I do. I believe you."

She smiled slightly. "But you don't know if you love me."

"Do you love me?" I asked.

Her smile stayed small, guarded. "I'd like to. But I worry."

"You worry about what?"

She frowned. "Time."

"That we don't have enough of it?"

"Yeah. I guess that's it."

"But we're young. God, we just graduated from high school. We have all the time in the world. Gale, why are you talking this way?"

She lay back down, but with her back to me.

Her voice, when she answered, sounded as if it came from a distance.

"I don't know why, but I feel we're all cursed."

I wanted to ask her to explain.

More, I wanted to know why I suddenly felt the same way.

CHAPTER

9

The next afternoon, Saturday, I sat alone in my living room and thought of Gale. I couldn't think of anything else. My parents were at the movies, so I had the house to myself. I felt I could be content to sit there all afternoon and replay the events of the previous day. It was the most exotic videotape ever made, my laser disc memory of our final day at school. Even Shena's attempted suicide and Gale's late-night bout of melancholy did little to upset the sweet tape that continued to loop through my brain.

I felt like I was in love.

Then I experienced a surge of the strange energy. The magnet, where had I put it? I stood and went into my bedroom and brought it and the large page of letters out. I tried to steady the string before I began. I wondered what Mentor would think of last night.

"Do you want to talk?"

Yes. It swung clockwise.

"Do you want to do what we did yesterday?"

Yes and *no.*

"Spell out what you want to say," I said.

The words were spelled slowly but deliberately.

Get a tape recorder. You will now speak for me directly.

I felt nervous. "Do you think I am ready?"

It will take some practice. You will feel as if you are speaking your own thoughts and not mine. This will be partly true, since I will be using your nervous system to communicate. But relax and have no fear—you will not go into a trance. You will be in control at all times, yet, at the same time, you must let go in order for the process to occur. To help you do this I want you to sit comfortably with the tape recorder on, and take long slow deep breaths for ten minutes. Breathe through your nose. Do not hyperventilate, just breathe easily. At the end of this time sit quietly and you will feel an urge to speak. Just go with this urge and don't care if what you say makes sense. It may not at first. But soon you will slip into a flow and you will feel great peace descend. Then, when you have a question, you can ask it aloud and I will answer it in your voice. Once again, have no fear. It is only fear that can block the process. When you are with me, you are with yourself. In a manner of speaking, you will be home.

I considered for a moment. I could already feel a sense of peace. It gave me faith. There was a sweetness to Mentor's energy that I could not define.

"OK," I said.

I had a small cassette player in my room. After finding a ninety-minute blank tape, I popped it in and tested the attached microphone. It was working fine. Returning to the living room, I sat in my father's favorite chair and positioned the recorder on the adjacent end table. I crossed my legs and closed my eyes. I wanted to be as comfortable as possible, I didn't know how long Mentor would speak.

Yet I didn't really have much faith that this would work.

The breathing was very relaxing. I glanced at my watch at the start, but didn't time anything exactly. At some point I think I drifted off. I could have fallen asleep, but I didn't think I did. I became aware that I was unusually relaxed. Words suddenly popped out of my mouth without my anticipating them.

"You are ready to begin," I said.

Somebody said. Or was it me? My voice sounded much the same, maybe slightly deeper. For a moment I had to struggle to keep my eyes closed and stay relaxed. More words emerged from my mouth.

"You are ready to begin."

"Is that you, Mentor?" I whispered.

"Yes."

"But I feel like I am speaking."

"You are speaking."

"But how do I know it's really you?"

"Relax and let it happen. Let there be no concern. Certainty will come later."

"OK."

"What do you wish to ask?"

My state of relaxation was deepening. Once again I felt the subtle movement of energy around my head and at the base of my spine. It was soothing and seemed both electrical and magnetic in origin, and as my attention focused on it, I felt my breathing slow even more.

"Is this all real?" I whispered.

"Yes."

"It is not a prelude to madness?"

"No."

"But schizophrenics hear voices?"

"Do you hear voices?"

"No."

"Do you hear anything?"

"No. Just normal sounds."

"Then you are not schizophrenic. You are able to speak these words because you are entering a refined state of consciousness. In this state you do not have any awareness of things in particular, you simply have a heightened state of awareness. To make it more confusing, this is a state of non-knowing, where anything can be known. It is a state of innocence, and in that innocence you can recognize the faint impulse of this telepathy."

"Is this how people communicate on your planet, through telepathy?"

"Yes."

"Can you send a spaceship for me and let me visit your planet?"

"No. If you came here in a physical ship you would find my planet covered with molten lava. At your level of density, my planet is unsuitable for human life. We do not exist at your density. You are what is called third density. We vibrate at a higher level, a fourth density. Yet long ago we were as human as you beings on Earth are at present. At that time, this world was much like your Earth. But that was millions of years ago."

"So you have evolved beyond physical matter?"

"Yes. The physical system is but one of many,

although your scientists think it is all that exists. But soon, very soon, they will have to change their way of thinking."

"How so?"

"Groups like yours will begin to emerge. They will possess powers your modern physical theories cannot explain. Perhaps your group will be one that will have a positive effect on humanity."

"You speak of me as different from you. But yesterday you said we were the same."

"We are the same, and in a larger sense we are different aspects of an even greater entity. But you, Daniel, deep inside, are not truly third density. You are like me, fourth density. You have merely taken on the shell of third-density existence to serve the people of Earth. It is a great sacrifice for you to be on Earth."

I felt myself smile. "It wasn't last night."

"Your favorite illusion. I am pleased you had fun."

"So what you're saying is that when I die, I will be with you?"

"Yes. You will not only be with me, you will be me."

"I will be on your world?"

"Yes."

"Cool."

"Yes."

"Is Ortee beautiful?"

"There is beauty here beyond your wildest imagination. The joys of third density cannot compare to fourth-density bliss. Your greatest joy on Earth would seem like abject suffering to us."

"Do all people who die on Earth move into fourth density?"

"No. They must reincarnate many times before they

perfect themselves enough to move on to fourth-density experience. Between lives, however, they rest and enjoy and assimilate what they have learned in their previous lives."

"But what you are saying is that my friends are all fourth density, correct?"

"Correct."

"And we have incarnated to work as a group to help humanity?"

"Correct."

"What specifically will we do?"

"When you awaken to your inner nature, you will develop powers. You will use these powers to help people, to demonstrate to them that there is more than the physical reality."

"You hinted yesterday that we could misuse these powers."

"Yes."

"Is that likely?"

"All is possible. It is up to you."

"Can these powers be used to harm?"

"Yes."

"Why does humanity need our help?"

"Evolution is cyclical. Humanity as a whole is about to complete one cycle. To continue to progress, humans must begin to look within for truth, not just outside to science, or even religion or philosophy for that matter. All these institutions are products of early third-density society. To you they possess your highest truths and embody your fondest wishes, but from our perspective they are merely a phase of growth."

"It sounds like our group has an important role to play."

"Yes and no. As I stated yesterday, you are uniquely qualified to help humanity. But all are equal in the eyes of the One Infinite Creator. Do not think of yourselves as important, it is the surest way to distort the powers that will soon come to you. Be innocent like children, as your mind is now, and you will know what to do."

"Is Gale close to me on your world? I mean, is her counterpart married to you?"

"We do not have marriage at our level. We do not have bodies as you understand bodies, although we do have form. And all are close in this density, all are one."

"But is she special to you in any way?"

"You cling to your illusions. Be wary of them."

"Is it bad that I am with Gale?"

"It is neither bad nor good. It is inevitable."

"OK," I muttered. I wanted Mentor's stamp of approval, but I could see what he was driving at. As we talked, my euphoria kept deepening. I felt expanded, no longer inside my body. I felt as if I were floating. Yet I could still feel my hands, my arms, and my legs. In no way did I believe my free will was being infringed.

"Very good."

"What is very good?" I asked.

"You see how crucial free will is. Throughout the galaxy, those of a positive vibration will never infringe upon free will."

"That's nice." I paused. "Are there negative beings in the galaxy?"

"Yes."

"What are they like?"

"They are of many densities, like positive beings:

*third, fourth, fifth, sixth. The main characteristic of
them is that they infringe upon others' free will and
serve only themselves. They have no love. They exist by
enslaving others, while positive beings grow by helping
to free others. You have been born on Earth to make
humanity more aware."*

"Could these negative beings obstruct my mission?"

"They are trying to do so at this moment."

"How?"

*"They are trying to feed you ideas of self-
importance. When the false personality, or what you
call the ego, dominates, the positivity of any being
decreases."*

"So these negative beings are on the subtle plane?"

*"They are both subtle and physical. Fourth-density
negative beings are also among your people at this
time, in large numbers, equal numbers to the positive
fourth-density beings. To maintain free will in your
society, this balance is necessary."*

"Do I know any of these fourth-density negative
beings?"

"I cannot answer that question."

"Why not?"

"To do so would be to infringe upon your free will."

"I don't mind."

"I cannot answer that question."

"Do you honestly expect me to tell all my friends
that I am talking to a spaceman?"

"Yes."

"They'll think I've lost my mind."

*"Only at first. Remember, they, too, are spacemen.
Deep inside they will know you speak the truth. They*

have been waiting for this time to arrive, a time when you are all together."

"When should I tell them?"

"Soon. But first you must get them all alone and in a harmonious spot. Suggest a retreat into the mountains, beside a lake perhaps. You have just graduated, and it would be natural for you to take a short vacation. Do not talk about me beforehand. But when you are all together, late at night, speak a little of me and then let me come and talk to the group. Have them close their eyes and breathe as you have done. They will begin to feel the peace you feel now. In that state I will be able to briefly lift you and them into a higher state and give you a glimpse of this fourth density. From that point on, the inner nature of each member of the group will begin to grow dramatically."

"Will we all be enlightened at that point?"

"There are many levels of enlightenment. But, no, I would say you will just be beginning on the path to enlightenment. Many obstacles will still stand before you."

"How do we defeat these obstacles?"

"By moving into stillness, into yourself, into innocence. Then you will know what is the right course to take."

"Will negative beings try to mess up our retreat?"

"Of course."

"Can you stop them?"

"You must stop them. If all your obstacles are removed, your growth will be inhibited."

"I just can't see this working."

"You did not think you could speak for me, but here you are doing it."

"As long as you are not just a figment of my imagination."

"We are all figments in the One Infinite Creator's great dream. This creation, all densities, are merely parts of one vast drama. One day you will see that again, and all your pain will be swept away. The task ahead of you is important, but it is all a play as well. The more you see the play from the director's point of view, the closer you will be to wisdom."

His words touched me. "I like you, Mentor."

"I like you as well. Have you any more questions?"

"I want to think about what you've said. I will get the group together. Is one date preferable to another?"

"The sooner the better."

"OK."

"Go now in light and love."

"Thanks. Goodbye."

It took me several minutes before I was ready to open my eyes. My body processes had slowed amazingly. Even though I had been talking, I was hardly breathing. As I stretched, I reached over and turned off the tape recorder. I was anxious to rewind the tape and listen to Mentor again. Each of his statements had been precious to me, and not because they had come out of my own mouth.

I heard a knock at the front door. Standing, I briefly had to steady myself against a wooden cabinet. But as I strode toward the door, I felt myself leave my experience behind. Indeed, I felt very fresh and alert. Mentor seemed to have a good effect on my energy level.

Gale was at the door. She had on a short white summer dress, a yellow ribbon in her hair. She wore a little lipstick but no other makeup—she needed nothing. The light in her eyes danced mischievously.

"What have you been up to?" she asked. "I knocked twice ten minutes ago."

"I didn't hear you." I opened the door farther. "Come in, my parents aren't home."

Her eyes widened as she stepped inside and pinched my belly.

"Does that mean you want to have sex real quick before they come home?" she teased.

I gave her a quick hug. "I don't just have sex on my mind. I appreciate you as a human being as well as an instrument of pure pleasure."

"Wow! I like that description, it suits me." Her eyes were searching. "Show me your house, I want to see how the other half lives."

I showed it to her. It took all of five minutes. We ended up in my room, kissing on the bed. I don't know who started taking off whose clothes first, but soon we were both naked. To see all of Gale's body in the daylight was a spiritual experience. But she didn't let me stare at her too long as she pulled me under the covers and kissed me in a way I assumed only Gale could kiss. Of course, I had never made out with another girl in my life. Yet somehow I managed to stop the plunge into ecstasy long enough to ask what I thought was a pertinent question.

"I meant to ask this last night. Are we using any form of birth control here?"

She was amused. "You think I want your baby? You think I love you that much?"

"Well."

She poked me. "I take the pill. I took one this morning. Are you happy?"

"No." I pulled her close. "But I think I will be in a minute or two."

Later, after we made love for the second time, I dozed. Really, I thought I was only asleep for a minute, but when I opened my eyes Gale was gone. For a moment I had a terrible image that I had slept for an hour, and that my parents had come home and peeked in my room while we were lying naked together. I wondered if Gale was in the living room explaining to my parents that we planned to get married as soon as the preacher arrived. Sitting up, I pulled on my pants and hurried down the hall.

Gale was in the living room sitting in my father's chair.

She had a bedsheet wrapped around her, nothing else.

She was listening to Mentor's tape. Maybe not for the first time.

She turned it off when she saw me.

For what seemed the longest time, we stared at each other.

"I can explain," I said finally.

She shook her head. Her expression was serious.

"You don't have to," she said quietly.

"I was just goofing off."

"No."

I forced a laugh. "Sure I was. It's something I do when I'm trying to get ideas for a story. I talk to myself and tape the conversation."

"No."

I fidgeted. "I'm not crazy, you know I'm not crazy."

She set the tape player aside and held out her arms. "Come here," she said.

I did as she requested. I sat beside her in the big comfortable chair, and she hugged me and buried her face in my side. For a long time we sat like that.

"You're not crazy," she said finally.

"Yeah. I was just fooling around."

"No. Mentor is real. I know he's real."

I drew back. "What are you talking about?"

She stared at me with an expression that I could only describe as profound. Yet there is pain as well as joy in great depth of feeling, and it seemed to me right then that Gale shook with revelations she wasn't sure she wanted to share. Yet there was a calmness surrounding her as well, as if our very discussion were inevitable.

"I have sensed something similar to what you just experienced for over a year now," she said. "I wanted to talk to you about it last night."

"Why didn't you?" I asked.

She brushed the hair from my eyes.

"You were too anxious to get my clothes off," she said. But then she withdrew her hand and lowered her head. "I thought I was crazy."

"Has Mentor talked to you as well?"

"No. Not so clearly. But for some time now I have known I was a visitor to this world. That I had come here for a purpose. And that you were somehow connected to that purpose."

"I can't believe it," I whispered.

A faint smile. "You can't believe, Mr. Spaceman?"

I felt overwhelmed by how fast everything was

moving. By the direction I was moving in. I hugged her tighter; it felt good to touch her skin.

"I don't know what to do," I muttered.

Her head pressed against mine. "Do what you've been told to do."

"But what if he's wrong?"

"Then do what your heart tells you to do."

"I don't know what it tells me. Except to keep loving you."

"Oh, Daniel." She kissed my head. "You are my Spaceman."

CHAPTER

10

To my immense surprise, I had no trouble convincing the others that we needed to go away together for a few days. It seemed that all of them, including Shena, had been thinking the same thing. I wondered how much Mentor had been working on each of us. I was especially pleased that Shena was receptive. Her breakdown at Disneyland seemed a forgotten nightmare. It was Shena, in fact, who located our retreat cabin, a three-bedroom exposed post and beam affair on a back road off the main highway to Lake Arrowhead. The place bordered another, smaller lake, and Shena said the real estate agent had emphasized its isolation and serenity. I was impressed with how fast Shena had found the cabin. We chipped in to pay for it, but I believe Shena paid more than her share. She was clearly anxious to be alone with Jimmy for a spell. I hoped they could work out their differences.

As we turned off the main mountain road and cruised down into the heavily wooded valley and saw Crystal Lake for the first time, I felt a calm steal over me. The place was familiar; in fact, I felt as if I had dreamed of it for years. The smooth mirrorlike lake water called to me. If I stared into it at night, I wondered, would I see the mysteries of the starry sky? I had spoken only once to Mentor since he had given me my orders. I had brought the few supplies he had said would be necessary to awaken our Star Group. Actually he spoke of them as symbols of a deeper reality, not intrinsically important, but useful as tools to help our minds expand.

The whole valley appeared deserted. I was puzzled since it was Friday and the weekend was coming. Shena explained; she seemed to know a lot about the area.

"This is mainly a skiing valley," she said. "During the summer everyone locks up their houses. The lake is not large enough for waterskiing or powerboats."

"But it looks like you can fish on it," Sal said, admiring the lake. He enjoyed fishing. Sometimes he brought his rod out on his surfboard, along with his cigarettes. He had once caught a two-hundred-pound tuna from Huntington Beach pier and swore he had eaten the whole thing in a week's time.

"The fishing is supposed to be good," Shena said.

Sal was driving us into the valley in his van. "I would like to get a rowboat and go out on it," he said. "What do you say, Jimmy?"

"I would just as soon swim in it naked with my girlfriend."

Shena hesitated, then smiled. "I'm game."

"I'd just as soon swim in it naked with all the guys," Gale said.

"Hey," I complained.

"I'm not taking my clothes off in front of you guys," Teri said.

"You may as well," Sal said. "I've shown Jimmy and Daniel those nude photos I took of you."

"I had six of them blown up and plastered on my bedroom walls," Jimmy said.

Teri chuckled. "Fortunately I never strip in a room where there is a camera. For that reason I know your photos are probably of Gale."

"Hey," I said.

"Maybe they are," Jimmy muttered, casting Gale a quick look. Sal glanced at her as well, and I couldn't help noticing the disturbing dynamics. But Gale kept her gaze straight ahead and focused on the lake. I would have given a pretty penny to know what she was thinking right then. What night she was remembering.

When we reached the cabin, five-sixths of the gang set about unloading and exploring. They all wanted to get the best room. But I never cared where I slept, and I wanted to get out and stretch my legs. I set off by myself around the lake, still marveling at its serenity. It was the kind of lake where a stone could skip a dozen times, and I picked up a pebble and got it to jump more than six times on my first try. The body of water was a quarter mile long, half that wide, an almost perfect oval.

The smell of the surrounding pines penetrated deep into my lungs and cleared out years of accumulated smog. The simple act of breathing was invigorating. I had to ask myself why I didn't go up to the mountains more often. The city was *thick* third density. When the sun went down that night I knew I would feel closer to the heavens than ever. Stars no longer spooked me. They were like old friends since Mentor had appeared.

Ten minutes into my walk I came across an old man who looked like Santa Claus after a macrobiotic diet. He stood tall and erect, with a white beard that reached almost to his belt. Although it was warm, he wore a thick red Pendleton shirt and what appeared to be heavy wool pants. He looked healthy enough, but instinctively I felt that if I had met him a year earlier he would have been much more vital. His eyes were clear, but tired looking. The lines that fanned out from them had been eroded into furrows by hard times. Father Time was catching up with him, and when he nodded to me and opened his mouth to say hi I noticed he was missing a few teeth. Still, I felt drawn to him as I watched him standing on the shore with a fishing pole in hand.

"Catch anything interesting?" I asked as I came near.

He shook his head. "Naah. Just a few miserable bass. I threw them back."

"How big do they have to be for you to keep them?"

"At least a foot. You don't want to bite into the young'ns. All you get are bones stuck in your teeth for your trouble."

"Don't you take the bones out before you cook them?"

He spat near the lake. "Nope. Don't cook them much, either."

"You're a sushi lover. I should have known by looking at you."

He appreciated my comment; he wasn't a bad guy.

He nodded across the lake toward our cabin. "I saw you drive in. How long you planning to stay?"

"Just till Monday." I sighed as I glanced around. "But it's so peaceful here, I wish we could stay a week."

He nodded at the water. "It wasn't so peaceful here last January."

"Why? What happened then?"

"The Donner family always came up here during the winter. They loved to ski and hike. They owned the cabin you're renting—they might still own it for all I know. Anyway, they were here last winter from Christmas to the middle of January. As you might imagine, this lake is pretty darn solid by then. David Donner—he was their young boy—loved to go ice skating every afternoon. But I warned him and his dad to stay away from the lake because we'd had several warm days in a row, with the sun shining hard on the ice. It looked none too strong to me—I wouldn't walk out on it."

"What happened?" I asked.

The old man began to reel in a fish.

"It was January tenth, twelve-thirty in the afternoon, when David was out on the lake skating and the ice broke beneath him. I saw him fall in from my place over yonder. I had been watching him closely because I was worried when neither him nor his dad heeded my warning. But Mr. Donner was a brave man, and when his son crashed through the ice and disappeared he ran out onto the lake to rescue him. I ran out of my cabin and got to Mrs. Donner in time to stop her." He shook his old head. "I'm glad I was able to save her at least."

"Did they both die?"

"Darn shootin' they did. They both went into the frigid water, and once the ice started to break all around them there was no way anyone could get to them. We could see them both thrashing in the cold, it was a terrible sight. Mrs. Donner couldn't stop crying, I wrenched my back trying to hold her on shore. We weren't alone; there were others around that afternoon. But not one of us could rescue them and they were only a hundred feet out at most." He nodded to the lake. "We never did find their bodies."

"Even after the ice thawed?"

"Nope. The lake was dragged and them steel hooks grabbed nothing but mud and empty beer cans. They're both still down there somewhere. I just hope one day I don't catch one of their eyeballs with my hook and reel it in. That would make me sick to my stomach, it would. But I suppose the fish have already made many a meal of their soft parts."

I was horrified. "I hope they died quickly."

"It wasn't that quick." The old man nodded to my friends across the lake. They were still walking back and forth between the van and the cabin. "But don't let what happened then spoil your vacation. You'll have fun."

"I hope so." I was beginning to wonder.

"You had fun last time, didn't you?"

"I've never been here before."

The old man squinted. "Oh, I never saw you before, that's right."

I felt a drop of ice water on the back of my skull.

There are all kinds of deaths. Some quick, some very slow.

"Have you seen my other friends before?"

He nodded. "I've seen that van, that's for sure. And that tall black fellow."

Sal hadn't told me about this place.

Right then, all my friends were outside by the van.

"Do you recognize any of the others?" I asked.

The old man squinted in their direction.

"I can't be sure. But that blond girl there sure looks familiar."

Gale was the only one who could be described as blond.

"The one with the white pants?" I asked softly.

"Yeah. I think I know her."

My throat was dry. "When were they here?"

"Last winter. No, maybe it was last summer. I can't remember."

My voice sounded pitiful to my own ears.

"But you're sure you saw them here together?"

The old man stared at me. He was no fool, he knew what I was asking.

"Son," he said as he reeled in a miserable three-inch bass, "when you get to be my age it's hard to be sure about anything. But I might have a long talk with my girlfriend if I was you. Or you might not want to talk to her at all. It all depends on what you want to do while you're up here."

I understood the choices. The peace of the place was a lie.

Also, it held on to its victims. Not a good omen.

This weekend I could cook or drown.

CHAPTER

11

That night, while we sat on the porch and looked out at the lake and the emerging stars, I brought up Mentor. We had eaten an early dinner, so none of our bellies was stuffed. I thought that was important if Mentor was going to do some kind of meditation with us.

The day had been pleasant, despite my uneasy feelings about Gale's past. We had swum in the lake, fished from it, and also rowed on top of it. On a hike later in the day we found a couple of neat caves far back in the woods. One cave, in particular, seemed to dig deep into the mountain. But we had not explored it as far as we might have. I think we were afraid of running into a bear. Sal had a revolver with him, which seemed to comfort the others but bothered me. I had never been a fan of guns. Sal was given the revolver by his real father, he said, ten years ago. It was a .357 magnum, and Sal said it could stop a big bear if he hit the beast in a vital spot.

I eased into the subject of Mentor by bringing up aliens.

I pointed out the Big Dipper, which was not so clear as it would have been if the moon were absent. Briefly I wondered if the full moon would aid the awakening Mentor hoped to achieve. It seemed a remarkable coincidence to me that it was so bright.

"Astronomers say there are over six hundred million galaxies in the bowl of the Big Dipper alone," I said. "Those are just the ones we know about. If you think about it, that each of those six hundred million galaxies has as many stars as our own—and the Milky Way has four hundred billion stars in it—then it makes you realize how small we are."

Sal was enjoying an evening cigarette because none of us would let him smoke in the cabin. He sat close to the edge of the pier, in the moonlight, away from Teri and the rest of us. By the feeble light of a flickering lantern, Teri was sewing a blouse. Jimmy and Shena lounged together on a hammock, and Gale sat at my knee, waiting for me to spill my guts.

"I like to reflect on how large the universe is," Sal said. "It makes me realize how insignificant my problems are."

"I've always wanted to look through a telescope," Teri said. "Daniel, you're a nerd, why don't you have one?"

I smiled. "My answer for everything. No money."

"I feel differently about astronomy," Jimmy said. "As well as the space program. Neither does anything to help our society."

"A lot of technology came out of NASA," Shena said. "That's where we got microchips."

"We would have invented them anyway," Jimmy said. "Don't get me wrong, I like the pictures of Mars and Jupiter and stuff like that as much as the next guy. But I don't think any of it has any relevance to daily life."

"I think the best things in life have no relevance," Sal said.

"Yeah," Teri agreed. "I'd take a magical life over a practical one anytime."

"Ms. Corporate America speaks," Jimmy teased.

"I'm only making money to buy freedom," Teri said. "Otherwise, I couldn't give a damn about it."

"Same line half the brokers on Wall Street feed people," Jimmy said. "And they all work until their bodies explode. You want money because you want money, and basically there's nothing wrong with that. Money's a reality—we couldn't have got this place for the weekend without it. But outer space is outer space. What goes on out there is never going to affect any of us."

Had Mentor placed that line in Jimmy's mouth to get the discussion started?

"You're wrong," Gale said quietly. "Daniel has been directly touched by outer space. Something incredible has begun to happen to him. Tell them, Daniel, you don't have to be shy."

I fidgeted. I would have preferred more lead-in to the discussion, but everyone was staring at me *now*. So *now* it was. Gale had spoken so seriously that no one had made a wisecrack. Not yet anyway, but the night was young. I didn't know how to begin.

"What's been happening?" Sal asked when he saw my discomfort. "You're among friends, you can talk."

I stammered. "It's hard to know how to start. Well, let's see. You all probably know I'm fascinated by the supernatural and read everything that's published in the New Age and occult sections of bookstores. The other day I picked up a book on magnets, how they can be used to tap into the subconscious and the superconscious. The technique the author describes allows you to ask questions and to get answers and hopefully new insights. While using the magnet, I refined my technique so that I could get it to spell out words and not just yes or no. I began to get very specific answers, from a source that identified itself as extraterrestrial." I paused. "I know that must sound crazy."

Still, no one laughed.

"What did this extraterrestrial tell you?" Jimmy asked.

"This will be hard to accept—it's taken me some time to accept it. This being—he calls himself Mentor—said that all of us, the six of us, are extraterrestrials. That we have been born here to help humanity. But that in reality we continue to exist on a higher plane on a distant planet even while we walk around on this planet."

There was a long moment of silence.

"He told you all this while you spelled out words with a magnet?" Sal asked.

"Not exactly. I started with the magnet, but then he told me that I could just speak for him."

"How did you do that?" Teri asked.

I sweated. "I did some long, slow deep breathing and then he took over and began to answer my questions. I had a tape recorder running. I never went into a trance or anything like that, and I wasn't channeling. Mentor explained the process as a high form of telepathy."

"What planet is he from?" Shena asked.

"Ortee." I added hastily, "But that's just a name. It's more important to understand that he's from a higher plane of existence, and that he has contacted us at this time to help us."

"But he hasn't contacted *us*," Jimmy said. "He's contacted *you*."

"He wants to speak to all of you while we're here," I said. "It wasn't my idea to come here. It was his."

"He's going to telepathically contact us here?" Teri said, and she looked as confused as the rest of us. Except for Gale, of course, who continued to stare at me like I knew what I was talking about. I appreciated her support, even though it had been silent so far.

"He wants to lead us in some kind of esoteric process that will open us up and give us a glimpse of our higher selves," I explained. "I don't even know what this process is. But he asked me to bring some stuff this weekend: a copper sheet with an eagle etched in it; and four precious stones, a diamond, a ruby, a topaz, and a sapphire. I was lucky, Gale had the first two, and I was able to pluck a small sapphire from earrings my mother has. The topaz we had to buy, we got a small one downtown. I made the etching on the plate myself."

"So you've talked to this alien?" Teri asked Gale.

"I didn't talk to him directly," Gale said. "But I listened to the tape Daniel made of him talking."

"What did he sound like?" Jimmy asked.

"Like Daniel," Gale said. "He uses Daniel's voice

to communicate, but the words he speaks are beyond anything any of us could say. It's obvious as you listen to him that he cannot be human."

"What makes it obvious?" Sal asked.

"There is a power in his message," Gale said. "A rhythm in his sentences. It's hard to describe, you just have to hear him."

"I would like to hear this tape," Jimmy said.

"You can't," I said. "I didn't bring it."

"Why not?" Jimmy asked.

"He wants you to be introduced to him as innocents," I said. "I may have already spoken too much about him and should let him explain himself."

"Through you?" Teri asked doubtfully.

I hesitated. "Yes."

There was another awkward pause. Jimmy finally spoke. He was my friend and could see I was uncomfortable.

"How can you know for sure that you're not making all of this up?" he asked. "You say he speaks through you. If you are not consciously controlling your words, then it's almost certain your subconscious is speaking."

I nodded. "I've thought about that, I don't completely dismiss it, either. But you have to experience Mentor to understand why I think he is genuine. A wonderful peace comes in his presence. Like Gale said, he's able to speak on subjects I know nothing about. I honestly doubt my subconscious could do that."

"But we know nothing about him—even if he is real," Sal pointed out. "And you want us to allow him to subject us to an experiment of some kind?"

"Yeah," Teri said. "What if he's a demon?"

It wasn't going to be as easy as Mentor had indicated.

"He's not evil," Gale said firmly. "I trust him. Let him come and you can ask *him* your questions. Let Daniel do his thing and relax and keep an open mind. We can talk about this all night and get nowhere."

Gale's remark had a settling effect.

Clearly no one really believed in demons.

"What are you supposed to do with the stuff you brought?" Jimmy asked.

"He'll tell us once the process starts," I said hopefully. "The only other thing he asked me to add to what I brought was some dirt. I picked some up near that cave we explored."

The group seemed willing to take it to the next level. We sat in a circle on the floor of the porch and placed the copper plate in the center. I brought out my tiny bag of precious stones. It had been generous of Gale to tear apart her jewelry to give me her stones free of their settings. I just hoped I hadn't damaged my mother's earring beyond repair. But I didn't know how to arrange the gems, so I just set the bag to the side. Then I told the group to sit up and close their eyes and breathe slowly through their nostrils.

Once again the breathing relaxed me so quickly that I lost track of time. One moment we were starting and the next I was floating so peacefully that I almost forgot that I was surrounded by my friends. Of course I hadn't left my body; I was drifting through inner space, not outer space. I noticed a deep silence all around me, a palpable presence so loving that in that moment I had no doubt we were in the company of a being from the stars. Mentor spoke through me, his voice soft but powerful.

"*This is an interesting experiment, for all of us. For you to listen to these words, to have faith in these words, and for me to guide you to a place not far from here, but a place you have forgotten. A secret place not in space or time but in consciousness itself. But I want only to guide you, not control you. And I ask for only a few minutes of trust. When we are finished, you may decide for yourself whether you should have faith in the reality of this night. Faith without experience to support it is merely blind hope, and blindness will never lead to the truth.*

"*My name is Mentor. It is just a name that I chose because it means 'wise teacher' to you. We have no names on my plane of existence because we have no separation from one another. As I speak, I do not see you as separate from me. That is how I am able to affect your state of consciousness, by sharing with you my own state. In reality there is only One. Whatever is taught is always a distortion of One. If you like, you can refer to God as One.*

"*But I have not come tonight to speak much. I have come to share experience with you. There is an energy in your bodies that sustains you. You call this energy many things—the names do not matter. Suffice it to say that this life energy flows through your body through seven centers. These centers are like keys on a flute, and how you play them determines the quality of your life. In other words, if you can lead your life energy up through these centers, in the end you will come to the One, which is the purpose of human life.*

"*The first five of these centers are associated with five*

elements. When I speak of elements I do not mean hydrogen or oxygen or carbon. Your ancients described the matter that makes up your universe in a fashion not connected to your Periodic Table, and your modern scientists were not wise to discard everything these ancients knew. There is indeed earth, water, fire, air, and space in every object in the physical creation. I will not go into this in detail right now, but perhaps later.

"At this time I want you to remain sitting quietly with your eyes closed. I am going to ask Daniel to place each precious stone on the sheet of copper. I want the diamond at the top, the topaz on the right, the ruby on the left, and the sapphire on the bottom. A small amount of dirt I want placed at the feet of the eagle. You may do this now, Daniel. Do not worry that the movement or the opening of your eyes will affect your focus."

I did as Mentor wished and closed my eyes again. He was right, my incredible calm had remained. He continued.

"What you now have before you is something the ancients called a yantra—*a point of focus. The yantra I have had you construct is similar to the one the Hopis used before the white man came to this continent. The yantra is merely a tool of truth, it is not truth itself. The yantra and its many parts represent an archetype. It connects the bound mind to the higher mind. Let me explain its symbology and then we will begin.*

"The earth element is represented by the dirt. Water is denoted by the blue sapphire. Fire is the ruby, and because the sun makes the wind blow, the yellow topaz stands for the air element. The diamond is of course symbolic of that most subtle of all elements, the

akasha, space itself. The eagle upon which all these are supported is representative of that aspect that connects a mortal to his immortal soul. The copper plate draws each of these elements together. Gold would have worked better, but I understand gold is expensive in your society.

"This is the yantra, a tool to help you focus. To focus is not to strain, but to dissolve. When you dissolve you allow your higher self to carry out your meditation instead of your limited ego. As each of these elements is represented on the yantra, each is present inside you in each of your seven centers. Each element and therefore each center will dissolve as we proceed. Let us experience this.

"Now focus your attention on the base of your spine where the first center is present. This is the earth center and the energy that radiates from it binds you to the earth. As you bring your attention to this spot, you may feel some energy. Be with it, don't resist it. It is not necessary for you to mentally link this center with the earth element on the yantra. That will happen automatically."

Mentor was silent for several minutes. Clearly I felt some type of energy flow through the base of my spine. I didn't have to strain to keep my attention there; the process was addicting. Mentor spoke once again.

"Bring your attention to just below your genitalia. Here is your second center, which connects to water. Your body is primarily composed of this element, and it also binds you to this planet. Let your attention relax here for several minutes."

Again Mentor fell silent. My euphoria continued to increase.

"Bring your attention to just above your navel. Here is your third center, which connects to fire. Allow your attention to focus here."

More silence. It was growing deeper.

"Bring your attention to your heart, the fourth center, which is connected to air."

I felt as if I were rising up. Being sucked up by a divine force.

"Come to your throat. To space."

The sensation was definitely liberating.

My mind was expanding rapidly.

"Be between your eyebrows. Home of the subtle mind."

As my mind grew in size, it lost all activity.

I was aware but I had no thoughts.

"Rest at the crown of the skull. Be content. Just be."

I was dissolving. The *I* was being annihilated.

I heard no more. Daniel knew no more.

Yet it was as if I now knew everything.

CHAPTER

12

The next day hiking by myself in the mountains, I tried to sort out what had happened the previous night. The experience had been the most profound of my life, yet I could hardly remember it—and that was driving me crazy. There were only fleeting images in my head: vast blue-green planes; cyclones of colors spiraling into space; flying ships that were made of living matter; and strange glowing beings that flew through the heavens like angels. But beyond these images had been the exaltation of perfect peace and oneness.

Yet I could not remember what I had learned. Worse, I didn't even know what the others had experienced. When I had become aware of myself again, I saw them lying around me, sleeping peacefully. And that morning, over breakfast, when I asked to discuss our experience with them, they had shrugged and said that it had been pleasant, like a Technicolor dream. Obviously they remembered less than I did, but still had positive feelings about Mentor and his process. They didn't make fun of me in any way, yet I found their vagueness disturbing.

My solitary hike was to bring matters into some kind of focus. At least I got some exercise out of the failed attempt. But I was surprised, on my way back, to find that Sal had also gone out for a walk. Actually, he was hanging out by a stream, throwing rocks into the water.

Throwing *very big* rocks into the water—boulders actually.

I surprised him as I came up behind him. He jumped.

"Daniel!" he scolded as he removed his hand from the stainless revolver he had tucked into his belt. "Don't do that. I thought you were a bear. I could have shot you."

"Sorry. I was so intent on watching you play that I forgot to announce myself." I gestured to the rocks he had thrown in the stream. "What are you doing?"

"Getting a little workout. I didn't bring my weights because there was no room in the van, but I need to work out every day." He paused. "Is there something wrong?"

I sat down on a medium-size boulder. "No."

Sal smiled. "I love this place. I feel so good here. I slept like a baby last night."

"That's what I wanted to talk to you about, last night. At breakfast this morning you didn't say anything about Mentor." I paused. "Do you think it's all nuts?"

Sal sat and pulled out a cigarette. "Not at all.

There's something there, that guy sure can speak on profound subjects."

"But what did you feel after he led us through the seven centers?"

Sal lit his cigarette. "I just felt great, but I think I fell asleep somewhere in the middle."

"What's the last thing you remember?"

Sal considered and then shook his head. "I'm honestly not sure. I just know I had a bunch of psychedelic dreams afterward."

"But you feel good now?"

"Yeah." Sal stood back up and did a couple of deep knee bends. "What do you think of that?"

"I don't think you should go out for the cheerleader squad in college. What do you mean?"

He beamed. "My knee feels better than it has since I hurt it. You probably don't notice because I don't walk with much of a limp, but I always have some pain in my left knee. Now it's gone."

"Totally?"

"Yeah. I don't even feel a twinge."

"That's incredible. Do you think it has anything to do with last night?"

Sal was puzzled. "Why do you say that?"

I shook my head. "Never mind." I pointed at the rocks. "Those are pretty big rocks to be tossing around."

Sal measured me with his eyes, which made me feel uneasy. But it wasn't as if his manner was hostile, only elusive. I couldn't imagine Sal angry, especially not at me.

"What are you getting at, Daniel?" he asked.

I stood. "Nothing. Have a nice hike. I'm going back."

Sal didn't offer to accompany me.

I found another solitary explorer thirty minutes later—Jimmy. He was sitting by himself on a stone ledge, staring off into the distance. The sun was brilliant in the sky, and I missed having my sunglasses. Like Sal, Jimmy did not even notice me approaching. He didn't jump when he saw me, only flashed me a beatific smile.

"How are you?" he asked. He appeared to be drunk.

"Great." I climbed up on the ledge. "Where's Shena?"

"I don't know."

"What are you doing out here by yourself?"

"Grooving."

I sat beside him. "Are you stoned?"

He kept grinning. "I feel like it, but I'm not. I think your Mentor session did something to me."

He was a pleasant change from the others. Actually, Jimmy had already been out for a walk when I awoke. He was the only one I hadn't questioned.

"Tell me what's happening," I said.

It was his turn to look embarrassed. "I know this will sound crazy, but when I sit here and close my eyes I'm able to see things far away."

"What are you talking about?"

"I see things in my head. Things that I can't see when my eyes are open."

"How do you know these things are real?"

"Because I can see them! They have to be real!"

Mentor had mentioned that powers would manifest themselves.

"Can I test your ability?" I asked.

"I knew you were going to ask that. But don't give me a formal test, just go with me to see if the treasure is where I think it is."

"What treasure?" I asked.

"Somebody buried a bag of gold dust a mile from here. I can see it. I can see it even underground!"

I was doubtful. "Do you know how ridiculous you sound?"

Jimmy was offended. "Ridiculous? You told us last night about an alien from another planet communicating with you via some sort of telepathy, and you say that I sound ridiculous?"

He did have a point. "How are we going to dig up this treasure? We don't have a shovel."

Jimmy was already on his feet. "We won't need a shovel if I'm right. It's only three feet below the surface."

I stood and brushed off my pants. "If we find it do I get half?"

Jimmy hurried down the side of the ledge. "No. Ten percent."

I followed, not expecting to find anything. "You should be the business major in college, not Teri."

Jimmy led me a mile through the woods, maybe more. By the time we reached the spot, I was tired and thirsty. We had dead-ended against a rocky cliff, and there wasn't anything to mark the area as unique. Then Jimmy seemed to develop a confidence crisis. He paced up and down in front of the cliff while I caught my breath. The air was thinner here in the mountains. For a moment, as I held up my hand to shield my eyes from the sun, I thought I saw it turn slightly blue. But the effect lasted only a moment.

Jimmy suddenly let out a howl.

"I know where it is!" he said.

"Where?"

He pointed behind a brittle little bush. "There."

"If we dig there the roots will get in our way," I warned.

He was impatient with me and my attitude. "If we don't dig there we won't find the gold. Do you want your ten percent or not?"

"I just wish we had a shovel," I said, judging how hard the ground was.

Jimmy scoured the area. "We'll find some stout branches. This will be money in our pockets. I don't know why you're so negative."

"Probably because you can see the gold and I can't."

We set to digging ten minutes later with a couple of thick sticks that were of questionable aid. The ground was gritty with tiny pebbles. We could use the points of the sticks to loosen the soil, but we still had to scrape it out of the way with our hands. Within minutes my fingernails felt like they were coming off. Jimmy was digging harder than myself, he actually had blood forming under his nails. I tried to stop him, to take a break, but he was like a man possessed.

"You are such a wuss," he said.

I plopped back on my rear. "Call me anything you want. I just don't like pain."

111

He was feverish. "No pain, no gain, Danny Boy."

He had never called me that before.

The last person to call me that had been Gale.

"Jimmy?" I said.

"Yeah? I think another foot and a half ought to do it."

"Can I ask you a personal question?"

"Sure," he said.

"How well do you know Gale?"

"What do you mean?"

"I mean, do you know her better than I do?"

"I don't know. I don't think so. You're right, I'm starting to hurt, too."

"Then stop, we can finish later," I said.

"No way, I want this now. Why are you asking about Gale?"

"Well, I know you talk to her a lot."

"I never once told her you were interested in her. I told you I wouldn't."

"That's not what I'm asking. I was just wondering, you know, after Shena had her accident if you ever felt attracted to Gale?"

That stopped Jimmy. He stared at me.

"What kind of question is that?" he demanded.

I shrugged diplomatically. "She's a pretty girl. I just wondered if you ever thought of doing something with her."

"Doing what with her?"

"Nothing."

"Are you implying that I slept with Gale?"

"No."

"Because if you are, you're pissing me off. I'm your friend, I wouldn't do that to you."

"I know that." I hesitated. "But were you ever interested in her?"

Jimmy averted his head.

"No," he muttered.

"Jimmy?"

He looked up. "What did she tell you?"

"Nothing. I swear, I just got this weird feeling."

Jimmy needed to take a deep breath. "I asked her out once. Just once."

"When?"

"I don't know. I think it was last summer."

"But you were going with Shena then."

"Maybe it was after that. I don't remember."

"But you were going with Shena after that."

He snapped. "I told you I don't remember! And I just asked her out, I didn't actually go out with her."

I spoke carefully. "Was it after Shena's accident?"

He was far from comfortable. "Yeah. It wasn't long after." Jimmy shook his head. "Shena was in the hospital and hating me. She wouldn't even take my calls. And Gale . . . she had been there that night. She had been through the horror with me. She could understand what I was going through. Could understand that *I* needed someone to talk to."

"You could talk to me." I was thinking that during that time I had talked to him an awful lot about Gale, and consoled him while he wept about Shena. But he was absorbed in himself and kept shaking his head.

"Gale was there. She helped me through a bad time."

"But you never went out?"

He threw me a hard glance. "We did not go out."

My anger showed. "You mean like you didn't get a pass from the principal to screw her? Is that what you're trying to tell me?"

Jimmy jumped up. "I don't have to take this crap from you."

I got up slowly. "You knew I was obsessed with her. You're a popular guy, you could have had any girl in school. Why did you have to hit on her?"

He fought to control his temper. "Nothing happened between us. We just talked. You can ask her if you don't believe me. In fact, I don't care if you believe me or not. You have no right to accuse me."

"Nice speech. Friend." I turned away. "Goodbye."

He grabbed my arm, panic showing on his face. His words spilled out.

"Don't go, Daniel." He put his other hand on my shoulder. "I'm sorry, it was a lousy thing to do and I know it. But I didn't do it to hurt you. I did it because I was weak."

I held his eye. "What exactly did you do because you were weak?"

He looked away, and I died a little right then.

"Nothing," he muttered.

"You didn't sleep with her?"

"No."

"You can tell me the truth. I would rather have the truth."

He stared down at his invisible buried treasure. "We just talked. Nothing more. I swear to you, Daniel. You have to believe me."

I stood there. Felt the hot sun. Felt my hot blood.

"I believe you," I said flatly.

Jimmy was relieved. He patted me vigorously on the back.

"Good. I'll give you twenty percent. Let's get back to digging."

I don't know why I continued to help him.

Maybe I thought if we dug deep enough, I could bury him in the hole.

But we found the sack of gold dust at three feet.

CHAPTER

13

My walk back to the cabin took much less time than Jimmy's. The bag of gold dust weighed at least forty pounds, and he insisted on carrying it. Fine with me. With the goods actually in his hands, I didn't know if he was reconsidering my percentage and I didn't care. I had a bad feeling about his new power and how he was using it.

Gale, Teri, and Shena were sitting on the porch. Teri was wrapping sterile gauze around Gale's hand, the sight of which immediately brought out the protective boyfriend in me. But the girls laughed at my concern.

"I slipped on loose gravel while we were out walking," Gale explained. "It's only a scratch. It's Teri who insisted on making a big deal of it."

"It's a pretty bloody scratch," Teri said as she reached for white medical tape. "It was gross to clean the pebbles out of the flesh."

"Don't talk about flesh," Shena said. She spoke to me. "Have you seen Jimmy?"

I sat down, I was weary. "He's right behind me. But he couldn't keep up. He's carrying something heavy that he refuses to put down."

"What is it?" Shena asked.

"A bag of gold dust," I said.

They stared at me. "What are you talking about?" Shena asked.

"Jimmy and I dug up a forty-pound bag of gold dust." I paused. "Jimmy woke up this morning with amazing powers. He says he can see things far off in the distance. I believe him. He sure could see the gold a long way off, and it was buried."

Teri frowned. "You're joking, right?"

I sipped somebody's glass of lemonade.

"I'm not," I said. "That session we had last night has affected Jimmy and Sal in amazing ways. I ran into Sal while I was hiking. He said his injured knee is healed. At the same time he seems a lot stronger than he should be."

Gale looked worried. "Why do you say that?"

"He was working out—as he called it—with stones I don't think he could have picked up yesterday."

Teri giggled. "Yeah, right. My boyfriend has turned into a super-hero."

I leaned forward in my chair. "He has changed, Teri. You can talk to him about it when he returns. You can see Jimmy's bag of gold when he gets here. I'm not making these things up. They are facts. Now what I want to know is if any of you girls have noticed any differences. I quizzed you at breakfast, but that was a while ago and maybe something has changed since then. Shena? Anything?"

She considered. "I have felt sort of powerful since I

woke up. Not that I can lift heavy stuff, but I do feel a kind of inner strength deep in my gut."

"Can you do anything you could not do before?" I asked.

She shook her head. "No."

I turned to Teri. "How about you?"

Teri laughed. "Oh. I can fly through the air now. I have X-ray eyes. How am I supposed to answer a question like that?"

"Honestly," I said. "Have you noticed any change since last night?"

Teri hesitated. "No."

"Teri?" I insisted.

"I feel a little different. I wouldn't say powerful, but I feel a charge in my body. I don't know what else to call it. But I assumed it was from sleeping in the mountain air. I sure can't work miracles or anything like that."

I looked at Gale. There was red showing through her bandage, she must have hurt her hand worse than she wanted to say. But what else didn't she want me to know? We had slept together the previous night, but we had not made love because we were both zonked out. Sitting close to her now, it was hard not to reach out and hug her and kiss her. She seemed to read my mind because she gave me a sweet smile.

"I have sprouted wings," she said.

"You have always had wings." I paused. "Anything different?"

She considered seriously. "Like the others, I can't point to anything definite. But I woke up this morning feeling clear. Like a mental fog I had been carrying around for years was gone. Then, a few times today, I have known what someone was going to say before it was said."

"Intuition," I muttered.

"That's your department," Gale said.

I sat back and shook my head. "Mentor said powers would develop in each of us. Who's to say they cannot overlap?"

Teri was doubtful. "You're saying what we did last night made a big difference?"

"Yes," I said.

Gale sighed as she put her uninjured hand to her head.

"I take back what I said a moment ago," she said. "I don't feel so clear right now. When I slipped and fell I landed on my butt and I think the force jammed my spine into my skull. I feel a nasty headache coming on. It hurts much more than my hand."

Teri was sympathetic. She set down the medical tape and put her hand on Gale's forehead. Sal said Teri had the greatest hands in the world. According to him, she could give a massage like nobody else. Teri softly stroked Gale's forehead while Gale sat back and closed her eyes.

"You might want to lie down and rest," Teri said soothingly.

"Hmm," Gale murmured. "That feels good."

"I'm sorry," Shena said to me. "I don't know if that much happened for me last night. I liked listening to that guy you were talking for and all. I got real relaxed and felt peaceful. But then I think I passed out. I don't want to hurt your feelings, Daniel, but I didn't have any major revelations."

"You're not hurting my feelings. I didn't have any

revelations, either." I paused. "At least none that I can remember."

"So *you* don't feel any different?" Shena asked, and there was an edge to her question that I found odd. She was staring at me intently with her right brown eye. Her left eye, which had been permanently stained a yellow color, drooped off to the side. She was losing motor control in it, possibly from lack of use. It was difficult to sit beneath her scrutiny and not think about her face. Indeed, Shena was studying me closely; it made me uneasy.

"I have a ton of images and feelings inside me that I can't put together," I said carefully. "A part of me feels I glimpsed Mentor's home world last night. I know that sounds crazy, but that's how I feel."

Shena seemed disappointed. "What was it like?"

I shrugged. "I can't remember."

Gale opened her eyes and sat up. Teri took back her hand.

"I feel better," Gale said suddenly.

Teri smiled. "I'm glad."

Gale paused. "No. I mean, my head feels perfect."

Teri flexed her fingers. "Sal says I have the magic touch."

Gale put her uninjured hand to her head. "You sure do. It's amazing."

My girlfriend—dare I call her that?—seemed stunned.

"What is it, Gale?" I asked.

Gale frowned. "Something changed in the last minute. It's weird, I can't . . ." She paused, and then began to unwrap her bandage. Teri tried to stop her.

"Don't do that, dear," Teri said. "You have to let it

heal. It's a scratch but it can become infected just the same."

Gale shook her head. "I want to see it."

The blood on the bandage made me not want to look. I had never been good with blood, it always made me sick to my stomach to be around it. Yet I continued to watch because Gale was clearly confused about something.

As she pulled the gauze away, we gasped.

There was blood on her hand but only on the surface.

Her scratches were gone.

"Wow," Gale said. "It healed." She turned to Teri. "You healed it."

Teri pulled back and shook her head. "I didn't do anything."

"But I felt something when you had your hand on my head," Gale said. "Like a mild current going into my brain. Then my headache vanished and my hand got better. You can see my hand with your own eyes. You know how bad it was cut."

Shena's eyes were huge. "Can this be true?"

I tried to stay calm. "Did you notice any power flowing from your hands, Teri?"

Teri obviously did not want to be anointed the next healing messiah.

"No," she stuttered. "I mean, yes, I felt something. But I have felt it before when I worked on Sal."

"What did you feel?" I asked.

Teri shrugged. "Good old-fashioned vibes. I don't know what New Age people would call it. My hands always get warm if I rub someone. Only this time, when I had my hand on Gale's head, it got real hot.

It felt like it was burning. I would have said something, but I didn't think it was significant."

"Your healing gift was probably latent," I muttered. "Maybe all these gifts are latent. The session merely woke them up."

"I'm not a healer," Teri protested. "I'm a teenage girl."

Shena stood. "Can you put your hands on me?"

Teri stared at her uneasily. "Oh, honey, I can't help your face. I'm sorry, but I don't think that's possible."

Shena was animated. "Don't say that. You can help me. Gale had a bleeding wound and you healed it. My face has already healed. You just have to get rid of my scars and fix my eye. I know you can do it."

Teri shook her head. "Don't ask me that."

Shena slammed her foot down. "You have to help me! Somebody has to help me!"

I stood. "Shena. We have to examine this calmly."

She turned on me and her working eye glared.

"You want me to be calm? If she can heal me, then she has to heal me! It's because of you guys that I'm this way in the first place!"

"Shena," Gale said. "Sit down and relax. Daniel is right, getting upset won't help anything."

Shena ignored her and stepped to within inches of Teri.

"Put your hands on me, please?" she implored. "I can't go through life looking like this. I'll die if I have to."

Teri was scared. "The plastic surgery will help a lot. You have to give yourself time to get better."

Shena was hysterical. "I'm not going to get better! I need a miracle!"

I don't know why Gale and Teri appealed to me right then. I was no leader, I didn't know what to say. Perhaps they thought I had Mentor on tap in my brain. I wished I had; I felt anything but clear.

"If you want to put your hands on her, Teri," I said finally, "do it. We can see what happens."

Teri shook her head. "I know this isn't going to work. I know it in my heart."

Shena wept. "Can't you try to help me? Do you hate me so much that you won't try?"

Teri lowered her head. "No one here hates you, Shena."

Shena closed her eyes and trembled. "That's a lie. You all hate what's ugly. It's human nature."

Teri looked up. "OK. I'll try to help you. But I can't promise anything."

Shena knelt on the floor before Teri. She grasped Teri's hands, her own shaking with hope. It was pitiful to watch. If Shena did not get her miracle, I worried about the fallout. Across the lake, out of the corner of my eye, I could see the old man by the water.

I thought of all the pain that lay buried all around us.

Teri put her hands on Shena's face and spread her fingers over the scarred area. Both closed their eyes and strove for calm, but Gale and I couldn't take our eyes off them. The whole time I kept thinking that what we were doing was wrong. We needed to sit quietly, take stock of the situation. But already Sal was flexing his muscles and Jimmy was collecting gold. I felt as if I were on an asteroid spinning out of control through deep space.

Teri sat with her hands over the left side of Shena's

face for five minutes, and the seconds moved more slowly than those on a broken clock. Both sat still, yet both seemed to be straining. Finally a noise from the far side of the lake distracted Teri, and she opened her eyes and glanced over. Jimmy was returning with Sal, who was now carrying the ravaged leather bag that contained the gold dust. Even from a distance we could see their idiotic grins. Jimmy waved; he sure had a bounce in his step.

Teri took her hands off Shena.

Opening her eyes, Shena grabbed her friend's hands back.

"Don't stop!" Shena pleaded.

Teri was anxious. "Nothing's happening."

Shena's eyes were huge. A tear rolled down the side of her face. The scarred side. It was almost as if it were a drop of acid; her flesh twitched. There were no good vibes in the air. The situation could not have been more tense.

"You have to try harder," Shena said, almost choking on the words.

Teri fidgeted and glanced at me. "I'm sorry, the juice is not there."

Shena pounded Teri's lap. "Make it be there! Don't quit! Please don't quit!"

Gale stood and stepped to Shena. She put an arm around her.

"Let's not push this," Gale said softly. "Maybe Teri can try later, when you're both more relaxed."

Shena shook her off and jumped up. She went to scream something at all of us, but then the life seemed to go out of her and she sank down into a chair and lowered her head and wept quietly. Gale knelt and stroked her right arm. Teri clearly felt in a difficult spot.

"I'm sorry," she said again.

"It isn't your fault," I said.

"No heat came into my hands. I couldn't make it come."

"No one is blaming you," I said.

Jimmy and Sal arrived a minute later. They were both bursting with enthusiasm, so happy they didn't even notice that Shena was in a bad state. Sal dropped the bag of gold dust on the wooden table on the center of the porch. Eagerly Jimmy tugged at the stiff leather string that held the bag shut. In seconds a huge pile of gold dust stood on the table. It did not sparkle in the afternoon sun, but none of us doubted that it was the real thing.

"Who's the man?" Jimmy asked, obviously assuming I had told the girls how we had located it. "Who's the man?"

Sal slapped him on the back. "You're the man!"

Jimmy gave him a high-five. "I'm the man!"

Sal grinned as he looked around. "Isn't this an incredible day?"

"Why don't you guys have a seat," I said. "We have things to talk about."

Jimmy blinked as he surveyed our less than excited expressions.

"What's wrong?" he asked.

"Nothing's wrong," I said. "But we need to talk. Please?"

Sal was disappointed. "But what about this gold we found?"

"Hey, I found it," Jimmy interrupted. "It's mine."

"The gold isn't going anywhere," I said.

Jimmy and Sal shrugged and pulled up a couple of chairs.

"At least I could be congratulated on my find," Jimmy mumbled.

Once again all eyes were on me, even Shena's. I had started the ball rolling, I suppose it was natural for them to think I knew where it was going. My only worry was that there was a cliff up ahead that Mentor had not told me about.

As a preliminary, I brought everyone up to date on what I had observed: Sal's knee; Jimmy's supernatural vision; Teri's healing ability. Sal and Jimmy got excited about what had happened to Gale's hand, but I pointed out that the ability had not *yet* worked on Shena's face. When I was through I turned to Sal.

"Are you noticing anything else besides an improved left knee?" I asked.

He hesitated. "What do you mean?"

"I picked up that bag of gold for a moment," I said. "It was heavy. But from the other side of the lake to here you carried it like it was a bag of popcorn."

"I carried it part of the way back," Jimmy piped in.

Sal was annoyed. "What is it with you, Daniel?"

"I just want to know if you have developed extra strength in the last twenty-four hours?" I said.

Sal snorted. "Yeah. I'm Superman."

I persisted. "What is with *you?* Why don't you answer my question?"

Sal eyed me real slow as he had at the stream.

"I have noticed that I feel stronger, yes," he said finally.

"How strong do you feel?" I asked.

He shrugged. "I don't know, like I could play

football again and be a winner. Does that answer your question?"

"Honey," Teri said. "Daniel is just trying to understand what's going on. We all are, you don't have to snap at him."

"I don't like being interrogated," Sal said.

I sighed. "All these things that are happening sound good and somehow we are making a mess of them. Maybe I'm to blame, I don't know. Maybe I'm being too serious and we should just enjoy these miracles. But besides trying to figure out how each of us has changed, I want to discuss where we want to go from here. But I don't want to talk about it alone. These things are supernatural—I think we need supernatural input."

"You want to talk to Mentor?" Gale asked.

"Yes," I said.

Gale surprised me. "I don't know if that's wise, at least at this point. Another session might accelerate what is happening. Already we're having trouble controlling the changes the group is going through. I would rather we use common sense to plot our next move. We can always talk to Mentor later if we feel the need. There is no reason to rush anything."

I eyed her. My trust in her was not at an all-time high. The suspicion might have been an overreaction. I think she sensed that my feelings toward her were unsettled. Still, more than anything, even in the midst of everything else that was going on, I was still desperate to touch her.

"I disagree," I said firmly. "Mentor is the only one we can turn to for guidance. He is the only one who understands what is happening. How can we plot our next move using common sense? The idea is ridiculous. Common sense would tell us that none of these things is happening."

Gale did not back down from my strong words.

"I don't think Mentor is opposed to common sense," she said. "All I'm asking for is a break. Let the atmosphere settle. We have the rest of the weekend."

"I want to talk to Mentor," Shena muttered.

Teri watched her with worried eyes. "He's not a god. He can't make everything all right."

Shena stared at her. "You don't know that. Why don't you give him a chance?"

"I don't mind talking to Mentor," Jimmy said. "As long as he doesn't tell me I have to put my gold back in the ground."

"Sal?" I asked.

He shrugged. "He's a smart guy. Talking to him can't hurt."

"Teri?" I asked.

Her eyes were still on Shena. She sighed.

"I don't know," she said. "We might be playing with fire. Maybe we should talk to an expert on this type of phenomenon."

I snorted. "Where are we going to find an expert? In the Yellow Pages?"

"There are psychic researchers," Gale said flatly. She was not pouring tons of love my direction and I didn't care. I was sure that I was right. Mentor would speak and everything would be made clear.

"Fine," I said sarcastically. "Call one up at UCLA or USC. Have him get in his car and drive out here today to wire our brains up to an EEG."

"Daniel," Gale began.

"Mentor is on our side," I interrupted. "Talking to him cannot hurt us, it can only help. Let's do it, let's do it now."

There was an awkward silence, more shrugs, lowered heads. The vote was not as clean cut as I wanted, but it appeared I had the majority on my side. After using the bathroom and grabbing some lemonade, we settled in a circle around our yantra. Like the previous night, we started the session by taking long slow breaths through our nostrils. I was pretty uptight at the beginning. I didn't think I would be able to settle down.

Yet somewhere in the midst of the breathing, I lost track of my surroundings. Peace and expansion settled over me, and my mind went into observer mode rather than active-thinker. I didn't know if I was reaching up to the same level as the previous night or if the night was merely coming back to me. I think it was a little of both. Images of a vast colorful plane flooded my awareness, clearer than ever before. I saw huge vessels moving through the starry sky, and beings of light that seemed independent of gravity. Several of the latter converged on the ground beside a cluster of glowing flowers that could have been a hundred feet tall. They formed a conference of some kind, and I knew they were exchanging ideas about planet Earth and how much help it needed.

There were six of them.

I realized I was observing the Star Group.

Our final meeting before incarnation on Earth.

Then my mind seemed to fragment. I was still observing them, but I also became aware of the background of the meeting. Not the physical background, but the historical events that had led up to it. Over thousands of years many beings from this world had chosen to come to Earth. But at this time, because it was the end of a vast cycle of evolution, more were planning to come at once, not just this group of six.

Yet these six were not all from this world. One of them was an alien to Ortee; its light was distinctively different from that of the others. Especially around the heart, where it did not glow with the wonderful green radiance of the others. As I came closer, I realized that even though this alien was of fourth-density vibration, it did have a form of sorts.

It looked vaguely reptilian.

Understanding swept over me. This being was from a race that had long ago warred with Ortee and its people. It was from another portion of the galaxy, beyond which there seemed to be a metaphysical barrier of some kind. Yet it wanted to incarnate on Earth with the others to contribute to the Star Group. It communicated positive intentions, and there was no mistaking the power of the entity. As I observed, I realized that even without the green radiance it was brighter than the other beings.

I wondered who it was.

Which one of us it was.

I thought it might be myself.

Right then the random idea of an eighteen-year-old guy named Daniel Stevens brought me partway out of my deep state. I became aware of my body and that I was sitting on the porch of a mountain cabin with my friends. They were silent; they didn't seem to be breathing deeply. Words popped out of my mouth, words I hadn't anticipated.

"This is Mentor. You may ask your questions."

There was a long silence.

None of them had questioned Mentor before.

Jimmy stirred. "Can I keep my gold?" he asked.

"Is it your gold? Do you own anything in this world?"

Jimmy seemed to fidget. "I suppose not. But what I want to know is if I can use this power to find other treasures?"

"Why do you want other treasures?"

Jimmy paused. "I figure if I can accumulate tons of money I could do a lot of good for people who are less fortunate than myself."

"A noble idea. Why else do you covet wealth?"

Jimmy chuckled. "I suppose I wouldn't mind a big house in Beverly Hills. Is there anything wrong with that?"

"I ask these questions to clarify your motives in your own mind. I will let you decide what is the wrong and right use of wealth. On the other hand, to use your ability solely to gather wealth is not wisdom. The only true wealth is awareness. It is all you will take with you when you leave this world. Certainly, you will not be able to carry any bags of gold with you."

Jimmy sounded uneasy. "I don't think there's anything wrong with a little money."

"That is true. It is a question of where your attention is. Where is your attention, Jimmy?"

A long pause. "I don't know."

"Reflect on that."

"I will." Jimmy added, "Thank you."

"I have a question," Sal said. "Is it all right if I go back to playing football?"

"Why do you want to go back to football?" Teri muttered.

"Because I love football," Sal said with feeling, talking to his girlfriend now instead of Mentor. "When I got hurt I had to bury my life dream to be a big star. Just because I didn't whine a lot about it doesn't mean it didn't bother me."

"I know it bothered you," Teri said. "But who wants to spend the rest of his life getting hit by other grown men? Football is a barbaric sport. Don't you agree, Mentor?"

"Don't try to put words in his mouth," Sal warned.

"I am simply asking him a question," Teri said.

"What is the question? Should Sal play football? Is football a positive way to spend one's life? I believe you are all old enough to answer these questions for yourselves. A better question, Sal, would be to ask yourself exactly how you want to use your newfound gift."

"I understand what you're implying," Sal said. "Football may seem a trivial pastime to you out there on your space planet. But here on Earth it's a big thing, and I love playing it. It's my first and last big love."

"I thought I fit in there somewhere," Teri said. "I guess not."

"Teri," Sal complained. "You're twisting what I meant."

"Let's not fight with Mentor," Jimmy butted in. "I'll find plenty of treasure and buy a professional football team. Sal can play or coach, it doesn't matter to me."

"I have a question for Mentor," Shena said.

"Yes?"

"Can you heal my face?"

"No."

Shena took a breath. "Can Teri heal my face?"

"Not at this time."

Shena wept. "Why not?"

"There is a time in life for everything. You live through many lives so that you gain many types of experience. This wound you carry is a catalyst forcing you to turn inward. All suffering, in your density, is a catalyst. Do not resist it, rather, learn from it. You have a great deal, Shena, that you can learn during this period of awakening. Your will is strong, your third center. There is a great fire in you. You must learn to harness this strength and control it for the benefit of mankind. But the first thing you must rediscover is that you are not your body. Your body changes; the real you is beyond change. Look within and discover this truth and your suffering will cease once and for all."

Shena sobbed. "But I don't want to be ugly."

"Shena," Jimmy interrupted.

Shena jumped up. I heard her. My eyes popped open.

Shena stood over Jimmy. Fire in her eyes, not her third center.

"You did this to me!" she swore, her fingers pointed like claws to scratch his eyes out if she wanted. "You did it to me on purpose!"

Jimmy slowly got up. The session was over and I knew clearly right then that that was a tragedy. Everyone looked nervous. Jimmy tried to touch Shena, but she pushed him away.

"Calm down," he told her. "Now I can buy you the best plastic surgeons in the world."

Shena went ballistic. "You think you can buy me a face? What you destroyed cannot be fixed! What you did cannot be forgiven!" She swiped at the bag of gold and sent the dust flying across the porch. "You keep your goddamn money! You spend it on your next girlfriend! You use your new power for yourself! I don't give a damn. You are all damned!"

With that Shena ran from the porch and into the house.

We let her go; we thought it best.

But when we looked in the house she was gone.

CHAPTER

14

I became lost in the woods shouting Shena's name. The mess at the end of the session had disturbed me greatly. I felt responsible for the situation and was trying to salvage my conscience by searching the woods aimlessly. At least I recognized the fruitlessness of my hunt. I had no idea which direction the cabin was or if I was not covering ground I had already covered. My voice was getting hoarse. If Shena was listening she probably wasn't going to answer me anyway.

I checked my watch.

I had been looking for her for three hours.

The sun was getting low in the sky. To be lost in the woods in the dark—what a scary thought. No, I take that back. I did not know what scary was. I did not know that for every ray of beauty in the universe there was an equal element of horror. Mentor had said something about the need for balance in all things. All the good that had happened to me in the last week, all the joy and exaltation, was about to be canceled out in one fell stroke.

I stumbled across the stream where I had earlier in the day found Sal tossing miniature boulders into the water. The sun was falling low, but it was still hot. Going down on my knees, I pressed my lips to the stream surface and sucked hungrily. But then I noticed a strange color in the water. That red kind of fluid that has a bad habit of showing up in a crisis.

The stream ran with blood.

I found Jimmy a hundred yards upstream, around a bend. He lay facedown in the water, the back of his skull split wide open. The wound was caused by multiple blows—the gore was splattered, not crisp. I had never seen a friend's brains before, never even stopped to imagine what they looked like. But as I turned away and vomited, I couldn't help thinking that all I had known and loved of Jimmy had been stored in that messy gray matter. Now, exposed to the air, scattered on the current, it was as if Jimmy had never been. Smash his brain, obliterate his existence. I choked on my vomit as I choked on my grief.

"Oh God," I wept.

I didn't know how long I stood there puking out my guts. It might have been ten minutes or an hour. I only knew that when I looked up, the sun had darkened in the sky. Everywhere I looked was black, even when I stared up into the blue sky and wept to Mentor and screamed why. The stars would never look the same to me from then on, I knew. I would see only the void between them, never the pinpoints of light, the rays of hope. At the sight of Jimmy's mutilated body, I felt as if the very purpose of humanity had vanished.

I didn't know what to do. To leave him seemed a sin, yet I knew I could not carry him back to the cabin. I had a sense of where I was now, and I was at least two miles from Crystal Lake. Trying not to look at his head, I flipped him over and dragged him by his feet out of the water. His pale washed face caught my eye, and I was relieved to see his expression appeared to be peaceful. The terror that had been inflicted on the back of his head did not register on his face. He could have been sleeping, I told myself. Yeah, right, sleeping with the worms. I couldn't imagine that we would have to bury him eventually, like any other corpse. He was my friend, he was supposed to be my friend all my life.

"Oh Jimmy," I moaned. "What did we do to you?"

Pulling off my shirt, I covered his head.

My walk back to the cabin was a funeral procession. I felt as if I carried his soul over my broken heart. That it swore at me from the spiritual dimension. The idea that he was once more happy on Ortee refused to stay in my mind. Right then, I felt Ortee had been the instrument of his death.

But I wondered who had killed him.

So many blows. So sadistic.

I ran into Gale at the halfway point.

"Oh no," she gasped when she saw my face. Falling into her arms, I felt sobs as heavy as thunder shake my body. I could not stop crying, I could not stop remembering. Not only his gory skull but all the good times as well. The brilliant memories were as painful as a river of red. It would have been far better, I thought, just to pretend I had never loved him. Love to me right then felt like the most insidious poison. Mentor was right about one thing: everything in the universe changed. Everything that could be loved would one day die. How useless a feeling, that it had been cursed by God from the beginning.

Gale shook me by my shoulders.

I forgot, she did not know.

"What happened?" she begged.

I tried to breathe. "Jimmy . . . he's dead. His head . . . his head is split open."

Gale shook her head. "No. Daniel? No."

I nodded miserably. "It's true. He's dead."

She collapsed in my arms and wept. "But it's not possible. He was just with us. He was just alive."

I couldn't comfort her. "We have to tell the others."

Gale pulled back. "No. Not yet."

I was comprehending so little. "Why not? They have to be told."

Gale bit her lower lip. "No. We have to think. We have to figure out what happened."

My brain was not working. "You think one of them killed him? No."

"It had to have been one of them."

I did not want to hear. "You're crazy, we're all friends. We're all friends!"

"Shh," she said. "This is serious. You know it had to be one of them."

I spoke like a wounded child. "Why does it have to be?"

"Because the chances of a stranger stumbling across Jimmy and killing him on this of all days is next to zero."

She had a point. "But none of them would kill our Jimmy."

Gale frowned. "You're sure he's dead?"

"Oh yeah. Someone pounded his skull."

"Someone strong?"

"What are you getting at? No!"

"Daniel! You have to stay with me right now. We're in trouble. We might be killed next. Sal is the strongest one in the group. You're the one who told us he's developed supernatural strength. He has to be considered a suspect."

"But Sal loves Jimmy. Sal loves everyone."

Gale shook her head. "Sal has been acting weird all day."

"What do you mean?"

"I don't know. Our whole group has been acting weird. Ever since that session."

"That's not true," I protested.

Gale was annoyed. "Yeah? Then why is Jimmy dead? Remember, he's the one who found the gold."

"Sal would not have killed his friend for money. No matter how shook up he was."

"Then why don't you come out and say it?"

"What?"

"That you think Shena killed him."

Her remark stunned me, not because it was incomprehensible, but because it was logical. After all, Shena had cursed Jimmy before disappearing. And where had I found Jimmy's body but in the only direction she could have taken.

Yet I shook my head once more.

"Shena could not do such a thing," I said.

"Then Teri did it. Then I did it. Are you satisfied with us as suspects? Daniel, you're the one with inner strength. I have not known you long, but I know that strength. Please, be strong now. Look at this situation objectively."

I had to hold my head. I felt it would explode.

"We need to sit," I mumbled. "We need to talk to Mentor."

"No," Gale said firmly. "I warned you not to have another session this afternoon and look what happened. From now on we're dealing with things in a practical manner. We have to figure out who killed Jimmy, and we have to go to the police with the culprit. If we can't decide, then we tell the police to arrest them all."

"But the police will never believe what has been happening here," I said.

Gale started to shout at me but stopped. She sighed.

"You're right," she said. "But we will still have to tell them about Jimmy. We can't go to jail over this. I don't mean to sound cold."

"You're not being cold. You're being strong. All right, let's look at the facts. Who was out of sight when Jimmy died?"

Gale groaned. "All of us. Teri stayed back at the

cabin in case Shena returned. Jimmy went chasing Shena, I went chasing you, and I don't know who Sal went after. But as far as I know we've been scattered all over the forest for the last three hours." She paused. "Could you tell how long Jimmy'd been dead?"

"I don't think it was for long." I shuddered. "Blood was still seeping from his head."

She grimaced. "Poor guy. This will break his parents' hearts. He's an only child."

"How well do you know his parents?"

"Well enough. Why?"

"No reason." I paused. "I honestly don't think it was Sal."

"You're not being objective. Sal is the only one of us who would have the strength to overpower Jimmy."

"Power is not the main issue. Motive is more important. Shena had her life ruined by Jimmy. The last we saw her she was screaming at him. If it was one of us, it was probably her."

"Probably is not good enough. We have to know."

My brain was in knots. "We're not going to know by standing here and talking. We need facts. We need to get back to the others."

Gale's eyes glazed over as she stared back the way I had come.

"You left him out there?" she whispered.

"Yes. I covered him as best I could."

"With your shirt?"

"Yes."

A tear ran over her cheek. "I really cared for him. He was a wild guy."

"Did you love him?" The question just came out.

She stared at me strangely. "No, Daniel. I didn't know him that well. What are you asking me?"

Her red eyes held mine, but I didn't have the strength to probe deeply.

"Nothing," I said.

We hiked back to the cabin in silence.

CHAPTER

15

Teri and Sal were waiting for us on the porch. Sal was panting hard; he did not look calm. Teri was sewing a blouse; I couldn't imagine anyone sewing after they had just committed murder. They both stood as we approached. Sal literally had rivers of sweat running down his body.

"Did you find her?" Sal asked.

"No," I said.

"Where's Jimmy?" Teri asked.

Gale and I looked at each other.

"He's dead," I said in a flat voice.

Teri coughed. *"What?"*

"Someone beat him over the head back by a stream," Gale explained. "They split open his skull. His body's still there."

Teri staggered and sat down. Sal did not jump to her side. He would not take his eyes off me.

He swore quietly. "This is a bad joke."

"No joke." I stepped on the porch. "Where have you been the last few hours?"

He was bitter. "Jimmy can't be dead!"

"Where have you been?" I repeated.

There was pain and fury in his face, an unpleasant brew.

"How dare you ask me that!" he snapped. "I've been out searching for Shena, like you and Gale."

"Did you get back right now?" I asked.

Teri was crying but I could not help her.

Sal glanced at his girlfriend. "A few minutes ago."

"Why were you running?" I asked.

"To hell with you!" Sal yelled. "If Jimmy's dead, I want to see his body. Gale, did you see his body?"

"No," she replied. She put an arm around Teri's shoulder.

"Believe me, he's dead," I said. "Why did you run all the way back?"

Sal was breathing hard. "I didn't run all the way. Are you saying I killed him?"

"Did you?" I asked.

He did not snap. He lowered his head. "No."

"All right," I said. "Maybe Shena killed him. It's possible. Until we're sure, can I hold on to your revolver?"

Sal took a step back. "Over my dead body."

"I don't want the gun in order to execute you," I said.

Sal reached behind him to his belt. So he had been carrying the gun with him.

"You're not taking my gun," he said.

"Why not?" I asked.

"Because you think I killed Jimmy! Christ, maybe you killed him! You're the one who's been talking to aliens! Who the hell knows what's gotten into your brain?"

"I didn't kill him," I said.

"Are you sure?"

Turning, I was surprised to see that Teri had asked the question. She was still teary, but she had mastered herself. She was a strong young woman.

And she was accusing me.

"My mind is clear," I said calmly. "I didn't kill anybody."

Teri held my eye. "But you're the only one who saw the body."

"Teri," Gale interrupted. "Daniel could not hurt a fly."

Teri nodded tightly. "I know that. But what about this Mentor dude? Sal is right, he's been taking over Daniel's brain. Maybe Daniel killed Jimmy and doesn't even realize it."

The idea should have been unsettling. But I refused to let it penetrate. I told myself that I had to hold on to the facts. And nothing could be set down in stone in my head if my mind was leaking fluids. Like Jimmy's head, the horror of his smashed brain almost engulfed me right then. I would have vomited had I anything left inside me. I met Teri's gaze.

"I didn't kill my friend," I said. "I would never have hurt Jimmy under any circumstances. You know that."

Teri nodded. "And you know Sal wouldn't have, either. So stop accusing him. We have to find the real killer."

Sal shook his head. "We already know who the

killer was. Shena has hated Jimmy since the night he accidentally fried her face. That hate has never gone away. We've all seen it. She sneaked up behind him and whacked him on the head—it's the only explanation." He drew out his revolver. "We have to find her."

Teri stood. "A crime has been committed. We have to go to the police. That's all we have to do. Let them take it from there."

"Ordinarily I would agree," Gale said. "But Daniel brought up an important point. No one is going to believe our explanation of what has gone on here. I wouldn't believe it if I hadn't been here."

"What are you suggesting?" Teri asked her.

"That we find Shena ourselves," Gale said. "Sal has the only gun. She won't be able to sneak up on us the way she did with Jimmy. We'll stay together and watch each other's backs."

"I agree," I said. "That's crucial. We stay together."

Teri shook her head. "I don't like this. Where are we going to look for Shena? She could be anywhere."

"We know she must have fled into the woods, probably in that direction." Gale pointed. "Daniel found Jimmy's body in that direction. Now, it's getting late, but if Shena stays in the woods tonight she'll have to seek shelter. Other than these cabins, where is there shelter around here?"

Sal gasped. "The caves we saw!"

I nodded. "She would probably head that way, it's logical. But I don't like the idea of going after her in the dark. We only have two flashlights."

Sal fingered his revolver. "I don't care if it's pitch

black. If she killed Jimmy, I want her brought in. Dead or alive."

"Hush that kind of talk!" Teri snapped. "We're going to find her. We're not going to shoot her. For God's sakes, we don't even know if she's guilty."

"Sal, I would prefer you didn't bring your gun," I said.

"Are you crazy?" he asked. "My gun is the only protection we have from her. I'm not going to stumble around in the dark without it."

"Daniel," Gale said softly. "Sal might be right. We might be better off having a gun with us."

"So you trust him now?" I asked, thinking of the old man's comments.

Gale did not flinch. "I don't know who to trust anymore."

CHAPTER

16

The sun was setting behind the horizon when we started on our hunt. Not for the first time did I feel like circumstances were spinning out of control. More than anything I wanted to close my eyes and be with Mentor, to know what was the perfect thing to do. But Gale's remarks made sense. It was Mentor's sessions that had triggered the tragedy. Chasing through the trees after Shena did not feel like the wisest course of action, but I could not decide what else to do. My intuition was a joke. My brain felt full of mud.

Yet I refused to consider that I was crazy.

There was no blood on my hands.

There was none on my clothes.

Of course, I had left my shirt to be soaked in blood.

We reached the stream and Jimmy's body, and there was a fresh round of tears. I tried to remain stoic, but Sal was in a rage. He screamed at the moon, and I thought if Shena was within twenty miles she certainly heard him. His insanity seemed to be an equal mixture of grief and hatred. He had his gun out again, and he was talking about how the bitch was going to pay. Good old Teri, what guts, she slapped him in the face and told him to get a grip.

"You're not going to bring Jimmy back behaving like a damn fool," she swore. "Daniel's right, you should hand over that gun to one of us right now. You're in no condition to be walking around armed."

Sal was adamant. "I'm not giving up my gun, no way."

"Then calm down and act like a man." Teri gestured to Jimmy's body, and she could not hide the shudder that went through her. "I wish there was more we could do for him right now."

"The best thing we can do is avenge his death," Sal said.

"Stop that!" Teri yelled at him.

Sal yelled back. "If she wasn't guilty why didn't she return to the cabin? Answer me that!"

"Let's stop fighting and find her," Gale said. "The police will come for Jimmy's body. Better we leave the scene of the crime untouched."

We started out once more. Sal fell behind with Gale. It sounded like she was trying to calm him down. Teri walked up front with me. I had one flashlight, Sal the other. Even with our battery-powered aid, and the moon rising into the sky, it was difficult hiking through the woods at night. Each odd-shaped shadow seemed to lunge at us. Several times we halted because one of us thought we saw something that wasn't there. Our nerves were not merely on edge, they were on fire. Teri fretted as she strode beside me.

"Do you know where you're going?" she demanded.

"I have a pretty good idea where the caves are," I said.

"This is insane."

"You won't get any argument from me," I said.

"Why don't we just go straight to the police?"

"We've been over that. How can we explain what's been going on here?"

"Why do we need to explain?"

I sighed. "We couldn't even begin to tell them the things that led up to Jimmy's death." I paused. "That reminds me, where's the bag of gold dust?"

"Back at the cabin."

"Where exactly at the cabin?"

"I don't know, you'd have to ask Sal. He hid it somewhere."

"He hid it? Why didn't Jimmy hide it?"

"Jimmy went chasing after Shena, remember? And you ran after them. Jimmy didn't have a chance to put it away."

"But Sal did," I muttered.

"Would you stop that kind of talk?" She glanced over her shoulder. Gale and Sal were fifty feet back, so they couldn't hear us. Nevertheless Teri spoke in a hushed tone. "You cannot honestly believe Sal would hurt his friend over a bag of gold?"

"If you had asked me yesterday, I would have said no. But today he's behaving like a loose cannon. I don't understand it."

"Maybe your alien session messed him up more than you realize."

"Maybe," I admitted. Yet that did not make sense

150

to me. All I had ever brought away from the sessions with Mentor was peace and love. How could such qualities lead to our current situation? The more I pondered our dilemma, the more it occurred to me that there must be an unseen element at work in our group.

I remembered the reptilian alien. So powerful.

Was it me? Or was it Shena?

The scars on her face looked scaly.

"Shena was furious, but she's not a cruel person," Teri said.

"But she almost killed herself at Disneyland. If she could do that, we have to assume that she could kill someone else. Also, Sal asked the question of the night. If she is innocent, why hasn't she returned to the cabin?"

"She might have got lost out here," Teri said.

"It's possible. Tonight, anything is possible."

We reached the deepest cave, the one we had been afraid to explore fully earlier in the day. Twenty minutes had elapsed since we had passed Jimmy's body. The tunnel went way back, but we noticed a faint orange glow in its depths. Somebody had made a fire in there. Somebody was planning on spending the night.

We huddled near the opening.

"She's probably in there," I whispered.

"Of course she's in there," Sal grumbled.

"If we sneak up on her, she might react badly," Teri warned.

"I don't want to announce our presence," Gale said. "If she's the murderer, surprise is our best weapon."

"She's going to hear us coming," I said.

"Not if I go in there alone," Sal said. "I'm quiet on my feet and you know I'm not easy to see in the dark."

"You're the last person who should go in there," I said.

Sal was intense. "I think *you're* the last person."

"I thought we all agreed to stay together," I protested.

"I'm having second thoughts about that," Gale said. "We assume we have the only gun, but I've been wondering how Shena could have taken Jimmy by surprise. Maybe she had him at gunpoint when she killed him."

"He had been beaten, not shot," I said.

"It makes no difference," Gale said. "She must have had him immobilized. She could have had a gun to his back and ordered him to stand still and then beaten him over the head with a heavy stone. My point is that for all of us to just barge into this cave and hope we get a friendly welcome is silly."

"You're scared," I snapped.

"I am scared," she said. "I'm the first to admit it. I would rather send in a strong man who is well armed to deal with a potential murderer than go myself. Let Sal go. He won't hurt her unless she tries to hurt him."

I was frustrated with her. "You change your tune quick. You have a little chat alone with Sal and suddenly you trust him to be a hero. Why, not two hours ago you were trying to convince me that he was the murderer."

Gale was angry. "That's a lie. I pointed out why Sal might be a suspect, nothing more. But now that I've talked to him his ideas seem the most logical."

Sal nodded. "There's no doubt in my mind that she killed him. We can't handle her with white gloves."

Teri was in a panic. "Last week you risked your life to save her, Sal. Now you want to track her down like a wild animal? What has gotten into you?"

Sal hissed, "My friend was alive last week! Now you guys stay here and let me do my job." He pulled out his revolver and took a step into the cave. "I'll not harm her unless she forces me."

I grabbed his shoulder. "I'm going with you."

He shoved me back. "You're all talk, Daniel. You're no good at a time like this."

I should have gone after him but I didn't. If a sequence of mistakes can be rated, that was the biggest one right there. But there was something in Sal's eyes—I thought if I pushed him too hard he might turn the gun on me.

The three of us waited by the cave entrance. We prayed—I did at least. But I did not know which God was listening tonight.

The fiery orange glow seemed to flare.

We heard a single shot.

"Sal!" I screamed. Not waiting for the others, I raced into the cave. The orange glow seemed to fade with each step I took. Yet it did not go entirely out, and I was able to reach the end of the cave without stumbling. There I found a medium-size space, as large as my parents' living room. It was roughly circular, with a ceiling barely above our heads. In the center on the floor was a small campfire, and I briefly wondered how such a small fire could have generated such a spasm of flame.

The walls of the space were scorched black.

Shena lay on her back by the campfire with her eyes shut.

Blood poured from her lower right side.

Sal stood over her with his gun in his hand. He was as pale as a black hole frosted by a galactic winter. All the blood in his face had drained into the hands that clenched the revolver. He could have been in shock. Carefully I stepped to his side and slowly undid his fingers from the gun. He did not hand it to me, but he did not resist, either. He kept staring at Shena, at the blood as it formed in a puddle beside the crackling fire.

I knelt and checked her pulse.

Both respiration and heartbeat were faint.

"She's alive," I said. "We need to get her to a hospital right away." I tore at my shirt. I sure was going through them. "We have to stop the bleeding."

Sal seemed to come alive. "I can carry her."

I stopped him from touching her. "Why?" I asked.

His mouth hung half open. "She tried to burn me."

"What?"

"I had no choice. She tried to burn me."

The girls entered the room. Gale was all business. She knelt and pressed my torn shirt onto the bubbling wound. Teri went to Sal's side but neither spoke. Slipping the revolver into the back of my belt, beneath what was left of my shirt, I tried to ease Shena up.

"Ohh," she moaned. But she did not regain consciousness.

Sal had to carry her, however. He was the only one who had the strength. He threw her over his shoulder like she was a sack of potatoes and hiked furiously out of the cave. We had to scramble to keep up with him, and he had a hundred and fifteen pounds on his back. All the time, of course, I knew we were behaving like fools. Sal had shot Shena and now he was trying to save her. But there was no time to sit and explore his motives, Shena was bleeding. With Shena riding on Sal's shoulder, we could not keep pressure on the wound to slow the blood. Gale did the best she could, stuffing our makeshift bandage under Shena's shirt.

It looked like Sal had shot her through the liver.

The hike back went quicker than our outward hunt. Sal was possessed with the strength of five men, and he practically ran with Shena. I staggered by his side and was stunned to see how openly he was weeping.

"How did she try to burn you?" I demanded at one point.

"I don't know," he gasped.

"Did she swipe at you with a burning stick?"

"I don't know!"

I had the gun. I figured we could find out the truth later. Our patient was all that mattered. Yet as we approached the cabin I had another dilemma to solve. Should we drive farther up the mountain, toward Big Bear, or head back down into the city? As the others hurried toward the cabin and the van, I took a detour toward the old man's cabin. As far as I knew he was the only other living soul around the lake.

"I need to ask where the nearest hospital is!" I shouted. "Swing around the lake and pick me up."

"We don't have time!" Gale shouted back as we split up.

"We'll lose more time driving in the wrong direction!" I yelled. "Do what I say!"

The old man did not answer my frantic knocks.

"Hello!" I yelled.

No response. I stood undecided for two minutes. Then, checking the doorknob, I discovered the place unlocked. As I stepped inside the dark cabin, a faint foul odor touched my nostrils. I stumbled over a coffee table and bumped into a lamp. Turning it on, I got another jolt in a night consumed by them.

The old man lay sprawled on his face in the middle of the floor. He was dead, the color of fish. He must have had a heart attack. There wasn't a mark on him. His flesh was cold, he could have been dead since the previous night. Outside, Sal was blowing the van horn. I wanted to do something for the man, but I couldn't. Right then I felt as if nothing I did would make any difference.

In the van they wanted to know which way to drive.

"Down the mountain," I said as I settled in the back beside Shena. Teri was up front with Sal, Gale was on top of Shena, trying to keep pressure on the hole. Sal shouted back to me.

"Isn't there a hospital in Big Bear?" he asked.

"I don't know," I said.

"What did the old man say?" Sal demanded.

"Nothing," I said.

Gale looked up, her hands soaked in blood.

"This is not my fault," she said.

"I didn't say it was."

"It's not your fault," she said.

Responsibility could be divided up later, I thought.

"Can she talk?" I asked as I gestured to Shena.

"She's unconscious," Gale said.

"Can you tell how she's doing?"

"I'm not a doctor." Gale checked her pulse. "Her heart's beating and she's breathing. That's all I know."

"Are your hands getting tired? Can you keep pressure on the wound?"

"My hands are OK." Gale paused. "She's not bleeding much anymore."

"That's good."

"I don't think so," Gale said. "I think she's about bled to death."

I was stricken. "She can't die. I need to talk to her."

Gale looked at me and shook her head.

"I don't think that's going to happen," she said.

17

We didn't find a hospital until we were well out of the mountains and into San Bernardino Valley. We saw it from the 10 Freeway, a huge modern facility with a helicopter pad on top, and Sal immediately yanked his van onto the next exit ramp. Sal had done a wild eighty miles an hour going down the mountains, and it was a wonder we were still alive. The amazing thing was that no one was screaming at him for shooting Shena. But the night was still young. I knew the cops would not be too happy to hear that a big powerful athlete had thought it necessary to put a bullet in an unarmed girl.

The hospital staff was efficient. We were twenty seconds at the emergency door when a swarm of medical people wheeled out a gurney and whisked Shena away. We followed them inside, but even though the nurses and doctors were shouting questions, they would not let us into the operating room. What could we say to their questions? She got shot. Who shot her? Gale and Teri held their breath.

I was the one who pointed Sal out.

We sat down to wait. Time crawled by as it had a habit of doing at times like this. Why didn't it know to slow down when times were good? God, I swore to myself, what a complete and total screw-up. The hands of the big white clock above us passed through an hour. I was sure someone somewhere was calling the police. Sal sat across from me, his head hung toward the floor. He quivered like a hurt child, and it was pitiful to watch him wring his big black hands. He did not want to look at me, but my eyes insisted. Gale was on my right, Teri on my left. In a sense Sal was all alone.

"Why?" I asked again.

His nerves were like parasitic worms eating him alive.

"I ran into the cave," he said. "There was a red glow up ahead. In the middle of it was Shena. I saw her, she saw me. Then a tongue of flame leaped out. She was trying to burn me. I didn't know what to do, I got scared." He shook his head. "I just fired. I didn't want to kill her."

Teri was worried. "Honey? What is this tongue of flame?"

Sal closed his eyes and shook. "That's what happened. Somehow the fire leaped at me. I thought she was doing it. I don't know what to tell you."

"You better know what to tell the cops," I muttered.

Teri gave me a cross look. "We should have gone to them to begin with."

"I think they'll be coming to us soon," Gale mumbled. Her hands were still bloody. She had not bothered to wash them. But I took the occasion to go to the rest room. Inside I splashed water on my face and stared in the mirror for a minute.

"Mentor," I whispered. "I don't believe you planned this."

My reflection did not reply. Or did it?

I took Sal's revolver and put it in the wastepaper basket.

I was not throwing it away. I was hiding it.

Yeah, the night was young and filled with promise. The missing element was still alive and well.

When I returned to the others, a nurse approached. She was young and pretty—she did not look much older than us. But her badge said RN Cathy Tiel. She had bad news, I could tell by the way her lower lip tightened before she spoke.

"Your friend has lost a tremendous amount of blood," the nurse said. "She's out of surgery and she's alive, but she's on total life support. She's being ventilated and has no brain wave activity."

Teri gasped. "Does that mean she's really dead?"

The nurse was blunt. "She will almost certainly not survive."

Gale and Teri wept. Sal and I must have felt we could not afford the luxury. Especially when the nurse pointed at us and told us to remain where we were.

"The police are here," she said. "Don't leave the hospital. They want to talk to you."

We sat back down. The chairs were not sturdy.

"God," Teri whispered. "We haven't even told them about Jimmy yet."

"We're going to have to tell them everything," Gale said.

I glared at her. "Now you like the idea."

She stared. "What's your problem? Do you see me blaming you?"

"We have to come up with a story," Sal mumbled. "They'll think I murdered Shena. They'll probably think I killed Jimmy as well."

"Did you?" I asked.

Sal was disgusted. "You're not going to walk away from this mess."

"Sal," Gale said gently, catching his eye. "We all know that you're stronger than normal. We're your friends. None of us wants to hand you over to the police. Screw what everyone else says. Do what you have to do to protect yourself."

"No," Teri interrupted. "We're not going to do anything except sit here and wait and talk to the authorities."

But Sal was thinking. "They ain't never going to believe me."

Talk about a walking time bomb.

His mumbling would light his own fuse.

A preposterous idea came into my head.

Energy came with it. Filling my whole body.

I turned to Teri. "We cannot sit here. You have to get in to see Shena."

Teri did not follow. "Why?"

"You have to heal her."

Teri drew back. "I can't do that. I couldn't help her face. The girl is practically dead. Daniel, don't ask me to do that."

I took Teri's hands. "We don't know how these powers work. Maybe they're stronger at times of crisis. I feel something incredible right now. It could be genuine intuition. All I know for sure is that there is something inside you that can make Shena better. But you've got to want to heal her more than you have ever wanted anything in your whole life."

Teri shook her head. "I can't."

I pleaded. "You have to try."

Teri wept. "No! You don't understand, I can't!"

"Why not?" I asked.

Teri looked down at her hands. "Because I'm afraid."

"I understand," I said, although I didn't know what she meant. "But if you don't go now, the police will be here. And they won't let us go so easily. You might not see Shena for hours and by then it could be too late." Leaning closer, I squeezed her hands. "Go to her, Teri. You're the only hope she's got."

A long moment followed, thick with turmoil and despair. Yet perhaps a ray finally shone from a distant star on our miserable group. A silent sigh seemed to pass through the air. Finally Teri looked up at me. Then she slowly nodded and stood. Stepping over to Sal, she gave him a brief hug and walked away. She did not say a word; we could only watch her go.

The police came for us five minutes later, specifically a plainclothesman and two uniformed cronies. Lieutenant David Madden was the name of the detective. His backup remained unintroduced. Lieutenant Madden was approximately fifty, with red skin and bad liver splotches. He looked like an ex-drunk who had sobered up on volcanic water. His gray eyes were hard and intimidating. He sat next to Sal after a quick hello and took out a notepad. He licked the tip of his pencil with his tongue, probably to sharpen it.

His hair was mostly white, his expensive sports coat a deep blue.

"What are your full names?" he asked.

We gave him our names. Lieutenant Madden wrote in shorthand.

"The name of the injured girl is Shena Adams?"

"Yes," I said.

"I understand she's in bad shape?"

Gale was soft. "They don't expect her to make it."

"That's a real shame." He was brisk but there was pain in his voice. But not for long, not as he stared at Sal. "Who shot her?"

Sal hesitated. "I did," he whispered so softly it was hard to hear.

"What did you shoot her with?" Lieutenant Madden asked.

"A revolver," Sal mumbled. "A three-fifty-seven."

"Your gun?"

"Yes."

"Where's that gun right now?"

"I don't know." Sal looked at me. "Didn't you take it?"

"No," I said.

Sal shrugged, he was out of it. "I must have dropped it in the cave."

"Which cave is that?" Lieutenant Madden asked.

Sal just shook his head. Gale spoke.

"It's in the mountains behind Crystal Lake, on the way to Lake Arrowhead. We drove here from there with Shena. We didn't know if there was a closer hospital."

"Is this the cave where Shena was shot?" Lieutenant Madden asked.

"Yes," Gale said.

"Did either of you two witness the shooting?"

"No," Gale and I said.

Lieutenant Madden put his hand on Sal's shoulder. "Why did you shoot her, son?" he asked.

Sal was having trouble breathing. "She killed Jimmy. She murdered my friend."

Lieutenant Madden frowned. "Who's Jimmy?"

"A friend from school," I explained. "I found his body earlier in the day. It's still up in the mountains. Someone split open his skull. At first we thought that Shena must have done it. Jimmy and Shena had had a big fight earlier in the day." I paused. "But now we don't know who killed Jimmy."

Gale spoke quietly but with strength.

"Sal might have killed them both," she said.

Her words did not have a desirable effect on Sal. For a moment he stared at Gale as if stricken. She had put an ice dagger through his chest. Then he leaped up and he was suddenly a fierce animal broken free of a strangling leash.

"I did not kill Jimmy!" he screamed.

Both blue coats were on him in a second. They were trained men, they knew how to subdue a hostile suspect. But as they spun Sal and tried to pin his arms from behind, a most amazing thing happened. Sal threw them off—literally, the two cops went flying backward and skidded on the floor. Lieutenant Madden drew his gun and stepped forward, but Sal was already moving. He whirled and caught the detective with a hard fist on the chest. Lieutenant Madden was stunned—he stumbled backward.

Sal turned and ran up the long hall.

The older of the blue coats recovered to his knees and trained his revolver on Sal's back. "Stop or I'll shoot!" he shouted.

Sal did not stop. Maybe he could not.

The officer shot. But the bullet went into the ceiling. At the last instant Lieutenant Madden had yanked his fellow cop's gun upward. Nice move, a testament to the fact that not all cops were bloodthirsty or hated blacks. But the heroic gesture was wasted. The younger cop had drawn his gun as well and Lieutenant Madden had only two hands. This fresh-out-of-the-academy sharpshooter fired off a round in Sal's direction.

A splat of red appeared midback on Sal's white shirt.

Sal went down hard and sprawled onto the floor.

I shoved the cops aside and ran to Sal. He was face-down in a red puddle. He tried to raise his head up, but the wires in his spine had been shorted. I took his hand and the look of confusion and agony on his face broke my heart. His voice came out weak and choked with fluid. Blood seeped over his lips. The cop's bullet had exploded his lung.

"I didn't want to hurt anyone," he gasped. "Love you guys." He went down. "Love . . ."

He closed his eyes and lay still. Dead.

I looked up at the cops. "He was a wonderful person." My hand sank in a river of red. "He was my friend."

The police were confused. Things had not gone by the book. They could see the headlines already. Bad PR all around. The young cop was crying. Lieutenant Madden was trying to marshal his forces and send for a doctor at the same time. Of course there wasn't a doctor in the entire clinic qualified to resurrect the dead. Gale stood leaning against a wall and stared off into the distance. I stepped in front of her. Her gaze was zombielike but I knew she saw me. Superficial looks did not impress me anymore.

"Lousy weekend, huh?" I said.

She blinked. "What?"

"You called me a spaceman. You asked if I loved you. You screwed my brains out. You were fun to go to Disneyland with. And yes, I did have a crush on you for four years." I paused. "But I don't know you, Gale."

I walked away. Felt her hard eyes on my back.

The cops had a lot on their hands. They let me go.

Somehow I knew what I would find.

In an intensive care unit that was strangely deserted—must have been the gunshots that scared everyone out of the hospital—I found Teri sitting in a chair beside Shena's sleeping form. Teri was not actually sitting—she had collapsed over Shena's chest. Pulling Teri upright, I had to shake her to get her eyes open. Her expression was worse than dazed, it was ashen. Her lips moved but I could not understand her words. I had to lean close.

"Sal?" she whispered.

She was not strong enough for the truth.

God knew what was wrong with her.

I forced a smile. "He's fine."

She raised a finger and wiped away a tear from my face.

And I had forgotten the blood on my hands.

Her eyes cleared. "He's gone."

I shook my head. "No."

She winced in pain and nodded. "I have to go."

I caught her as she slumped to the side. "What's happened to you?"

Her dreamy smile caught me off guard. She touched my chin. Her touch was so soft, it could have been an angel's caress. Her fingers were on fire, but it was a soothing heat.

"Oh, Daniel," she said. "It wasn't your fault."

It was too much to bear. "Teri?"

Her eyes closed. "You did not know."

Then she died. In my arms, she was no more.

I picked her up and laid her on a nearby bed.

I returned to Shena and held her hand. Her side was heavily bandaged. She had a tube stuck down her throat and one up into her bladder, and a dozen wires draped around her head. But I knew any second she would open her eyes and be OK. Teri was an angel; she had not left without giving us a gift.

The scars on Shena's face were slightly better.

Teri had given understanding as well.

I had much to tell Shena.

CHAPTER

18

The present moment is the same endless nightmare. Only that is not precisely true. This, the longest of all nights, has finally finished. While I typed, the sun rose over the city. I am back in my bedroom, at my desk. My parents are away for the weekend. My computer is hooked up to the telephone line. My modem dumps this story across town into Shena's computer. I wonder if she is home yet. Or on her way over to my house. I had told her to turn on her computer the moment she got in. Not that it matters; her online service will store this file for future reference.

Yet I hope Shena is coming over.

There is a sound outside. It must be either Shena or Gale.

I will go see. I take the gun . . .

It is Gale. She now sits across the room from me, on my bed, where we made love one week ago. She tells me I am to keep typing and I do what she says. Not that I want to, but I feel I must obey her. A peculiar magnetism swarms over my head. Sal's gun rests beside my computer. Gale doesn't seem worried about it. Before leaving the hospital, I snuck it out of the garbage can. The police were in such disarray.

Gale tells me to write down everything as it is happening. I doubt she knows about my modem wire attached to the back of my computer. I feel no compulsion to tell her, but if she asks I am sure I will confess. It is not visible from her position on the bed, and it seems there are some limits to what she can do.

She smiles at me. She has cleaned herself up. Her pants are burgundy, new, her blouse is white and tight. She does not wear a bra and I can see the shape of her nipples through the material. Her smile is sly but also slightly sad. The latter makes me wonder but not much. A snake cares for its newborn, but if starving will consume them. Gale licks her lips in that sexy manner she has perfected.

But I no longer want to kiss her.

"Are you writing about me?" she asks.

"A few observations," I say.

"You still want me. You still love me."

"No," I say.

Her eyes focus on me. "You'd better fix that. I don't want that in the story."

"I still love you," I say.

She sits back and relaxes. "That's better."

"May I ask questions?"

"Yes, Daniel. You may."

"Who are you?"

She enjoys the question. She knows I suspect the answer. It heightens her pleasure but not mine. Even though she has forced me to talk about love, I feel only revulsion in her presence. Certain illusions die hard, but this one has a stake through its heart.

"I am the balance on the scale," she says. "Five bright lights visit this world and I come to keep them in line. It only takes one of me, you know."

"You are the other?"

Her eyes are cold. "Yes."

"Have you always been able to dominate the will of others?"

"The ability was latent. Not fully manifest. I needed you and Mentor to activate it fully. I thank you for that. In a sense, I owe you."

"How long have you known what you are?"

"For a year I have suspected."

"Where are your adopted parents?"

"Dead."

"When did they die?"

"Recently."

"How did they die?"

"Very slowly."

"You spoke to Shena before we went on the Matterhorn?"

She nods. "I touched her mind. Pushed her."

"But if she had jumped, it would have messed up the Star Group?"

"You notice she did not jump."

"But you could have made it so?"

"Maybe not then. But now . . . of course."

"You knew I would gather the Star Group?"

"Yes. I knew you were the key."

"That was the only reason you slept with me?"

"You were good. You have pleased me."

"I am confused. What chance did we ever have against you?"

"You had every chance. But I slowly poisoned your apples before they could ripen."

"You planted dissension in our group. You seduced Jimmy?"

She grins. "And Sal. And Shena, don't be shocked. I had them all trembling with their secret sins."

"But Sal loved Teri. Shena and Jimmy loved each other. You could not destroy that love." I pause. "It was you who rigged the battery to explode in Shena's face."

"Yes. I killed Jimmy's battery, then used my car to jump it. My car battery is much larger. I switched the wires before I turned on my engine and gunned the accelerator. Shena had her face right over the battery." Gale pauses. "I took good care of her on the way to the hospital. I made sure the acid was not wiped off."

"Why did you have to destroy her face?"

"You said it yourself. All these acts weakened your group. Jimmy and Shena's love did not survive the scars; it does not matter what you say. Also, deep in your mind, on a subconscious level, I knew you would begin to associate Shena with the enemy if her face was scaled like a reptile's. When the moment of my attack started, you would be confused."

"Did the group on Ortee know your true intentions?"

Gale hesitates. "No. They were fools."

"But you're not sure about that?"

Her eyes flash with anger. She sits up sharply.

"You will not write that!"

"You are sure."

She relaxes. "Better."

"You pushed Sal all day yesterday?"

"Yes."

"You pushed him at the end to run?"

"Yes."

"Did you push the cops?"

"Cops are cops. It was not necessary."

"Did you kill the old man?"

"Yes. He was old. I stopped his heart with a thought."

"Looking back, I see that once you had the activation session finished with, you did everything in your power to keep me from being with Mentor."

"That is correct. I kept you from seeing the truth." She pauses. "It was right there in front of you all the time. You missed the biggest clue of all."

"What was that?"

"That a girl like me would chase a loser like you."

My face burns with blood. "What was it like to kill Jimmy?"

The topic is a favorite. "He was vulnerable when I reached him by the stream. He was worried about Shena, and at the same time he was gloating over his newfound ability. He thought he would be the richest man in the world. I was able to dominate his will completely. I made him keep his eyes open but his mouth shut while I pounded his skull. I insisted he stand up straight. I wouldn't even let him fall over. He had to stand there and watch his blood soak his shirt. He saw pieces of his brains." A casual sigh. "I took my time, I prefer to do so. He was not dead until he hit the water."

I hate her. "You're a monster."

She is not offended. "I am of negative polarity. It is not that I don't choose love; I cannot feel it. My power is therefore undiluted." She pauses. "The world will soon see more of my kind."

"You will be stopped."

She mocks. "Could you five stop me?"

I pause. "Teri shocked you."

She shrugs. "She threw her life away to save Shena. What a waste. I will get to Shena when it suits me."

"But Teri was strong. She gave her life energy for Shena."

She is not impressed. "Your type serves others. We serve ourselves. Our course of evolution is straight and clear. You get lost on tangents."

"I suspect your course is straight and barren."

"As you wish."

"What are you going to do to me?" I ask.

She gloats. "How did you start your story? Did you write something silly about having to kill yourself to make everyone safe on Earth?"

"Yes." I am staggered. "You put that idea in my mind."

She pities me. "Danny Boy. You *are* Mentor. If you kill yourself and go back to Ortee, you are not going to be able to influence matters here. You will not have a body." She pauses. "But you do not have to kill yourself. I give you a way out."

"I'm not interested."

She points. "Type with one hand. Pick up the gun with the other."

I do not want to. Honestly, I fight not to. But my strength is diluted.

I pick up the gun. She is serious now, she no longer smiles.

"Where does it hurt, Daniel?" she asks softly. That familiar gentle tone, always whispering in our brains. The gun shakes in my right hand; I can hardly type with the left.

"Please," I say.

Her eyes are like a snake's. They peer from the pit. There is not a trace of emotion in them. Why could I not see her soul in them before? She is right, I was a fool.

"Aim the gun at your right thigh," she says.

I fight her. I appeal to her. I beg.

"No, Gale."

She will not let me escape her dagger stare.

"Aim the gun at your right thigh," she repeats.

"No!" I cry. But I do what she says.

"Put your right index finger on the trigger."

I feel the trigger. The oil of my sweat. This cannot be happening.

"No," I whisper.

"Pull the trigger, Daniel."

"No!"

"Do it!"

I pull the trigger. There is an explosion of noise and pain. Red splatters my computer and my face. She does not let me close my eyes. I am not allowed to invoke the power of Mentor. I am alone here on Earth, in this bedroom, in this hell, with this demon. My right leg is a mass of gross tissue. I see my veins, my shredded muscle, my blood drips over the floor.

The agony is beyond imagining. I feel I will black out, I pray that I might. She regards me critically.

"Are you sure you're not interested?" she asks.

I choke on the horror. "What do you want?"

"You spoke to Shena after Teri healed her. I am sure she is out there up to no good. If you will tell me what you two planned, and then swear to me on your eternal soul to execute her at the earliest opportunity, I will let you live. Such a vow is important and binding. It will serve two purposes. I will be rid of her and I will have a fresh ally. Because if you join me, you will lose positive polarity. You will become like me and you will serve me for the next billion years."

My leg, my poor leg. She makes me keep looking at it.

"I don't believe I can lose my soul to the likes of you," I gasp.

She leans forward. "That is because even at this late date you do not comprehend what I am." She stops. "Put the gun in your mouth."

"Gale?"

"Put the gun in your mouth."

The gun is in my mouth. It tastes of gunpowder.

She is intent. "Do you wish to join me?"

I stare into her eyes. Satan's mirrors.

So much pain. God help me.

I shake my head. Jesus.

"Keep typing," she says.

I don't know how I do it.

She has the voice of a beast. "You are running out of time. You are alone here. No one is going to come to your aid. I am going to ask you one more time. If you refuse my offer, I will force you to pull the trigger.

Your brains will spray the wall behind you. The back of your skull will explode. Your mother and father will find you that way and it will destroy them. From now until the day they die their lives will be ruined. Neither of them will ever be able to get the image out of their minds of how you died. They will dream about it when they are awake. It will be like an open wound that cannot heal, and to make sure it never does, I will occasionally return to this house and remind them how their only son killed himself." She pauses. "You have to make a choice. You understand this?"

I nod. I type. The gun feels so hard.

She stands and looks down at me.

"Will you join me?"

I smell smoke. Somewhere near, something burns.

The odor distracts her. She momentarily turns away.

"Interesting," she mutters.

I am able to take the gun out of my mouth.

But I cannot turn it away from my face.

She comes back to me. She is not from the stars. She is a worm crawled out from the lowest cesspool. Her breath smells of decay, of all the future pain and death she will work on this fair planet. Yet I am no longer daunted by her stare. She can control my limbs, but she can no longer control my mind. Mentor is near; I feel the peace of my loving soul. It is one thing she cannot take from me.

"What is your decision, Daniel?" she asks.

I force a smile. I must give her nothing.

Finally I know contentment.

I will be with my friends soon.

Yet that does not mean I wish to die.

"You were lousy in bed," I say.

She is startled. *What?*

My smile grows. "The answer is no, bitch."

She is not happy. "Put the gun back in your mouth."

I have to do what she says.

Something worries her. She glances uneasily around.

There is smoke in the room.

"Pull the trigger," she orders.

I am sorry, I must do what she asks.

EPILOGUE

At the funerals for James Yearn, Sal Barry, Teresa Jettison, Daniel Stevens, and Gale Schrater over a thousand people turned out. Most were students from La Mirada High, but there were numerous adults and even several community leaders present.

The sudden loss of five promising young people had shocked the city. What made the pain particularly sharp was that there were still no answers from the police. Only questions and doubts and tears. The authorities said they would issue a definitive statement soon.

But there was one person at the funerals who knew they never would.

Shena Adams stayed by herself, her face covered with a heavy black veil. During the ceremony in the chapel she remained in the last row, and when the coffins were brought out to the grave site for final words and last goodbyes, she stood at the back of the crowd. She noted how small the coffins for Daniel and Gale were. The police had been unable to reconstruct much from the ashes. Certainly no one in the future would ever suggest that Daniel had killed himself. His shattered skull had crumbled in the high temperatures. No one would suspect Gale's role. The police had yet to find the bullet that had finished Daniel. The pieces of the puzzle lay in ruins.

And no one would ever read Daniel's computer files, unless Shena gave them a peek. She had a copy of Daniel's last story on a disk in her purse. His modem had been reliable. Too bad she had not reached his house in time, after reading the first pages of his story. At the hospital, when she had awakened after her healing, he had not understood the full extent of the danger. But he had been suspicious, and had told her enough. To be on her guard.

But not enough to save himself. When she had heard the second shot, she had known she was too late to save him. She had sent out her flames with total abandon. The full power of the third center, the secret prison of will. In the midst of her grief, it had been good to hear Gale screaming. And should more of her vile character appear on Earth, Shena knew how to deal with them.

The Star Group had been successful; she wished she could tell Daniel to his face. The enemy had been stopped.

The coffins were lowered into the ground.

The Valley of the Shadow of Death.

The rivers of star dust drifting between galaxies.

Shena caught up with Daniel's parents by their car. His father was a big man with gray hair and a gruff face. His brown eyes were warm, though they were much faded on this sad day. The mother looked like her lost son, with her innocent mouth and her long curly brown hair. Yet all was vanquished by her pain. Shena hardly knew what to say. She hugged them before she spoke.

"I am so sorry," she said. She would like to have confessed why she had not returned to the cabin after her outburst. How she had simply been too embarrassed. But they would not have understood, and besides, the act would not have stopped the demon inside Gale from striking.

Mr. Stevens nodded. "We're going to miss him. Thank God you were spared."

"Yes, dear. You must have a good life. For their sake at least." Mrs. Stevens broke down and wept. "He was such a good boy."

Shena's eyes burned. "He was the best."

Mrs. Stevens embraced her again. "Come see us some time, dear."

"I will," she promised. Then she pulled back her black veil and kissed the woman's cheek and whispered in her ear. "Daniel was filled with love. He was your son. You have much to be proud of. More than you know."

The woman seemed touched by her words.

Yet Shena's clear face confused Mr. and Mrs. Stevens.

"What happened to your scars?" Mrs. Stevens asked. "Your eye?"

Shena dried her eyes and smiled sadly.

"My friends healed me," she said.

———————————

Look for
Christopher Pike's

The Hollow Skull

and

Tales of Terror #2

Coming Soon

———————————

About the Author

CHRISTOPHER PIKE was born in Brooklyn, New York, but grew up in Los Angeles, where he lives to this day. Prior to becoming a writer, he worked in a factory, painted houses, and programmed computers. His hobbies include astronomy, meditating, running, playing with his nieces and nephews, and making sure his books are prominently displayed in local bookstores. He is the author of *Last Act, Spellbound, Gimme a Kiss, Remember Me, Scavenger Hunt, Final Friends* 1, 2, and 3, *Fall into Darkness, See You Later, Witch, Die Softly, Bury Me Deep, Whisper of Death, Chain Letter 2: The Ancient Evil, Master of Murder, Monster, Road to Nowhere, The Eternal Enemy, The Immortal, The Wicked Heart, The Midnight Club, The Last Vampire, The Last Vampire 2: Black Blood, The Last Vampire 3: Red Dice, Remember Me 2: The Return, Remember Me 3: The Last Story, The Lost Mind, The Visitor, The Last Vampire 4: Phantom, The Last Vampire 5: Evil Thirst, The Last Vampire 6: Creatures of Forever, The Starlight Crystal, The Tachyon Web, Execution of Innocence, Christopher Pike's Tales of Terror #1,* and *The Star Group,* all available from Archway Paperbacks. *Slumber Party, Weekend, Chain Letter,* and *Sati*—an adult novel about a very unusual lady—are also by Mr. Pike.

Christopher Pike presents....
a frighteningly fun new series for your younger brothers and sisters!

SPOOKSVILLE™

1 The Secret Path 53725-3/$3.99

2 The Howling Ghost 53726-1/$3.50

3 The Haunted Cave 53727-X/$3.50

4 Aliens in the Sky 53728-8/$3.99

5 The Cold People 55064-0/$3.99

6 The Witch's Revenge 55065-9/$3.99

7 The Dark Corner 55066-7/$3.99

8 The Little People 55067-5/$3.99

9 The Wishing Stone 55068-3/$3.99

10 The Wicked Cat 55069-1/$3.99

11 The Deadly Past 55072-1/$3.99

12 The Hidden Beast 55073-X/$3.99

13 The Creature in the Teacher 00261-9/$3.99

14 The Evil House 00262-7/$3.99

15 Invasion of the No-Ones 00263-5/$3.99

16 Time Terror 00264-3/$3.99

17 The Thing in the Closet 00265-1/$3.99

18 Attack of the Killer Crabs 00266-X/$3.99

19 Night of the Vampire 00267-8/$3.99

A MINSTREL BOOK

Simon & Schuster Mail Order
200 Old Tappan Rd., Old Tappan, N.J. 07675
Please send me the books I have checked above. I am enclosing $_____ (please add $0.75 to cover the postage and handling for each order. Please add appropriate sales tax). Send check or money order-no cash or C.O.D.'s please. Allow up to six weeks for delivery. For purchase over $10.00 you may use VISA: card number, expiration date and customer signature must be included.

POCKET
BOOKS

Name _____

Address _____

City _____ State/Zip _____

VISA Card # _____ Exp.Date _____

Signature _____

1175-17

R.L. STINE'S
GHOSTS OF FEAR STREET ®

10 The Bugman Lives!	52950-1/$3.99	
11 The Boy Who Ate Fear Street	00183-3/$3.99	
12 Night of the Werecat	00184-1/$3.99	
13 How to Be a Vampire	00185-X/$3.99	
14 Body Switchers from Outer Space	00186-8/$3.99	
15 Fright Christmas	00187-6/$3.99	
16 Don't Ever Get Sick at Granny's	00188-4/$3.99	
17 House of a Thousand Screams	00190-6/$3.99	
18 Camp Fear Ghouls	00191-4/$3.99	
19 Three Evil Wishes	00189-2/$3.99	
20 Spell of the Screaming Jokers	00192-2/$3.99	
21 The Creature from Club Lagoona	00850-1/$3.99	
22 Field of Screams	00851-X/$3.99	
23 Why I'm Not Afraid of Ghosts	00852-8/$3.99	
24 Monster Dog	00853-6/$3.99	
25 Halloween Bugs Me!	00854-4/$3.99	
26 Go to Your Tomb -- Right Now!	00855-2/$3.99	
27 Parents from the 13th Dimension	00857-9/$3.99	

Simon & Schuster Mail Order
200 Old Tappan Rd., Old Tappan, N.J. 07675
Please send me the books I have checked above. I am enclosing $_____ (please add
$0.75 to cover the postage and handling for each order. Please add appropriate sales
tax). Send check or money order--no cash or C.O.D.'s please. Allow up to six weeks
for delivery. For purchase over $10.00 you may use VISA: card number, expiration
date and customer signature must be included.

POCKET
B O O K S

Name _____

Address _____

City _____ State/Zip _____

VISA Card # _____ Exp.Date _____

Signature _____ 1180-23

DON'T MISS THESE GRIPPING PAGE-TURNERS

Christopher Pike

☐ LAST ACT	73683-3/$3.99	☐ MASTER OF MURDER	69059-0/$3.99
☐ SPELLBOUND	73681-7/$3.99	☐ MONSTER	74507-7/$3.99
☐ GIMME A KISS	73682-5/$3.99	☐ ROAD TO NOWHERE	74508-5/$3.99
☐ REMEMBER ME	73685-X/$3.99	☐ THE ETERNAL ENEMY	74509-3/$3.99
☐ SCAVANGER HUNT	73686-6/$3.99	☐ DIE SOFTLY	69056-6/$3.99
☐ FALL INTO DARKNESS	73684-1/$3.99	☐ BURY ME DEEP	69057-4/$3.99
☐ SEE YOU LATER	74390-2/$3.99	☐ WHISPER OF DEATH	69058-2/$3.99
☐ WITCH	69055-8/$3.99	☐ CHAIN LETTER 2:	
		THE ANCIENT EVIL	74506-9/$3.99

☐ THE WICKED HEART .... 74511-5/$3.99
☐ THE MIDNIGHT CLUB .... 87263-X/$3.99
☐ THE LAST VAMPIRE .... 87264-8/$3.99
☐ REMEMBER ME 2: THE RETURN .... 87265-6/$3.99
☐ REMEMBER ME 3: THE LAST STORY .... 87267-2/$3.99
☐ THE LAST VAMPIRE 2: BLACK BLOOD .... 87266-4/$3.99
☐ THE LAST VAMPIRE 3: RED DICE .... 87268-0/$3.99
☐ THE LOST MIND .... 87269-9/$3.99
☐ THE VISITOR .... 87270-2/$3.99
☐ THE STARLIGHT CRYSTAL .... 55028-4/$3.99
☐ THE LAST VAMPIRE 4: PHANTOM .... 55030-6/$3.99
☐ THE LAST VAMPIRE 5: EVIL THIRST .... 55050-0/$3.99
☐ THE LAST VAMPIRE 6: CREATURES OF FOREVER .... 55052-7/$3.99
☐ SPELLBOUND .... 73681-7/$3.99
☐ THE TACHYON WEB .... 69060-4/$3.99
☐ EXECUTION OF INNOCENCE .... 55055-1/$3.99
☐ CHRISTOPHER PIKE'S TALES OF TERROR .... 55074-8/$4.50
☐ THE STAR GROUP .... 55057-8/$3.99

Available from Archway Paperbacks
Published by Pocket Books

Simon & Schuster Mail Order
200 Old Tappan Rd., Old Tappan, N.J. 07675

Please send me the books I have checked above. I am enclosing $_____ (please add $0.75 to cover the postage and handling for each order. Please add appropriate sales tax). Send check or money order–no cash or C.O.D.'s please. Allow up to six weeks for delivery. For purchase over $10.00 you may use VISA: card number, expiration date and customer signature must be included.

Name _____

Address _____

City _____ State/Zip _____

VISA Card # _____ Exp.Date _____

Signature _____ 785-21